DISLOCATIONS

By the same author

The Ivory Swing
The Tiger in the Tiger Pit
Borderline

DISLOCATIONS

Stories by

JANETTE TURNER HOSPITAL

Louisiana State University Press
Baton Rouge and London

First published in Canada by McClelland and Stewart (Toronto), 1986
First published in Australia, with additional stories,
   by University of Queensland Press, 1987
Manufactured in the United States of America

97   96   95   94   93   92   91   90   89   88   5   4   3   2   1

Library of Congress Cataloging-in-Publication Data

Hospital, Janette Turner, 1942-
   Dislocations.

   I. Title.
PR9199.3.H596D5   1988   813'.54   88-9371
ISBN 0-8071-1508-8

Lines from "The Waste Land" in the story "You Gave Me Hyacinths" are
reproduced by permission of Harcourt Brace Jovanovich, Inc., from
Collected Poems: 1909–1962 by T. S. Eliot. Lines of verse quoted in the
story "Golden Girl" are from "The Lady of Shalott" by Alfred Tennyson.
The following stories have been previously published, sometimes in slightly
different form, as follows: "Happy Diwali," in *North American Review*;
"You Gave Me Hyacinths," in *Malahat Review*; "The Inside Story," in
Canadian Forum; "Waiting," in *The Atlantic*; "Ashes to Ashes," in
Encounter; "The Dark Wood," in *Dalhousie Review*; "Some Have Called
Thee Mighty and Dreadful," in *North American Review*; "After the Fall"
and "The Baroque Ensemble," in *Queen's Quarterly*; "The Owl-Bander," in
Canadian Fiction Magazine; "Golden Girl," in *Mademoiselle*; and "After
Long Absence," in *The Yale Review*.

The author gratefully acknowledges the assistance of the Literature Board of
the Australia Council.

The paper in this book meets the guidelines for permanence and durability
of the Committee on Production Guidelines for Book Longevity of the
Council on Library Resources. ∞

For Clifford, Geoffrey, and Cressida,
my fellow dislocatees,
with love

Contents

HAPPY DIWALI

HIS HIGHNESS IS HERE, of course. He sheds his nylon parka, a drab grey one, to reveal a satin shirt with splendidly billowing sleeves. It is the colour of fresh cream and has pearl buttons. His trousers, of grey flannel, are Etonian. Literally. He was already six feet two at public school and has not grown since. He would prefer not to be so frugal about his wardrobe but is running out of money.

Nalini Mahalingam, wife of the coconut-oil-and-papadam-importer, is here too. One expects to see her in furs, but no, she likes to experiment with the very latest and is wearing one of those quilted eiderdown things in a dusty pink.

I have always thought that padded and cross-thonged snow boots detract, in a rather serious way, from the delicacy of Kashmiri and Benares silk. But what is one to do here? The Canadian winter sets in early, giving no quarter, and one can hardly celebrate *Diwali* in anything other than one's costliest and most recently imported sari.

Namaste, namaste, we greet one another – or *namaskaram* – depending on regional origins and linguistic affiliations. Hands together before the face, heads momentarily bowed, like Norman Rockwell Christians at prayer. There are even some West Indian families who exchange what I suppose to be a calypso handshake and who are here, one must conclude, because they know which port their great-grandfathers were press-ganged from. Standards are slipping, but we need the membership dues. Already the Gujaratis are gathering in one corner and the Tamils in another. The Bengalis have put themselves in charge of the cultural part of the program and are busy organizing everyone else. The Delhi group, always drawing attention to itself, is pining in ostentatious Hindi for Connaught Circus. Only exile and isolation unite us.

The cloakroom (we have rented the auditorium of the local community college for the evening) is impossible, rampant with snow boots. They grow upwards, a tangled and fetid underbrush, toward the jungle of coats and dangling scarf creepers. Everywhere there is a steam of winter breath and damp mittens. One has to struggle, now, for hangers and space, plunging in between nylon and down thickets. I half expect to find Radha herself somewhere deep in there. The dankness, I suppose. The sense of rain forest and fungous murk.

New people keep arriving. As though it were part of the ritual, they place their Corningware casserole dishes – fragrant with Madras curries and Tandoori chicken and *kurmas* and *masala dosai* – delicately on the floor. For we are nothing if not small-town-Ontario and this is a pot-luck *Diwali*; which, I suppose, should be no more surprising than the fact that we are using electric candles instead of oil lamps. No doubt the goddess Lakshmi is sufficiently gratified to see her thousand lights bloom in an alien land, whatever the source of their flickering.

The bringers of casserole dishes peel off their Western layers of warmth, and lunge at the bloated coat racks.

Then: reincarnation.

Of course we are never surprised by it, not even those of us who grew up Christian. I watch the metamorphosis, gilded *avatars* emerging in a flurry of silks, cloth of gold, magentas, *salwar chemeez* as red as betel juice, blues exotic as Krishna's face or a peacock's breast. Colour, perhaps, is the last thing we let go of.

Two children, five-year-old Sikh boys with their uncut hair in little topknots, dart into the cloakroom shrieking with excitement. There is a sound of shattering. Ochre wavelets of lamb *biryani* lap at the snow boots and several people click their tongues in mild annoyance, stepping delicately aside. Someone nudges the shards of Corningware out of the way with one foot. No one thinks of reproving the children or of cleaning up. The fact that I think of these things is a mark of the extent of my displacement; and a measure of the embarrassing degree of sentimentality to which I will submit tonight. If I were to mention the mess, people would look vaguely puzzled. It is not a matter about which one should be concerned. There is always a *peon* to attend to that sort of thing.

In the auditorium, foil cut-outs of the Hindi letters for *Happy Diwali*, each about two feet high, are strung across the front of the stage where they dance gracefully in convection currents eddying up from the radiators. Old and solid, the radiators are the coiled water-circulating kind, metal sculptures in their own right. I think, with a terrible pang of longing, of the cast iron ornamentation of the Queen Isabella Hotel in Goa.

From across the aisle, His Highness, standing as though on guard for all that keeps slipping away between our fingers, inclines his head and upper body slightly toward me. I make *namaskaram* in response. I persist in South Indian ways, a pledge of allegiance. We are all of us addicted to nostalgia, and it is here, at the annual celebration of *Diwali* (a Hindu festival alien to both of us, strictly speaking), that His Highness and I give way to our addiction. We indulge. We lay in (to use a metaphor of Canadians, which is what we now are, if documentation is anything to go by) we lay in, as it were, supplies of the necessary mythic warmth against the coming winter.

His Highness, Prince Sana'ullah, is actually the great grandson of a ruler who was deposed by "a wicked cousin" well before the abolition of the princely states, those "dark places of the earth," as Kipling called them, the numerous tiny feudal kingdoms that dotted pre-Independence India. The prince's great-grandfather was not merely deposed. He was beheaded. This has cast a permanent aura of romantic tragedy upon his descendants, and naturally even the wicked cousin and his successors felt obliged to see to it that all family members lived and were educated in a style befitting Moghul royalty.

But then the privy purses were abolished (though not of course before certain sums had been removed to England and Switzerland against just such contingencies). Prince Sana'ullah was given his obligatory British public school education, following which he was asked by his father, who had his own lifestyle to maintain, to consider life in the colonies, where both royalty and public school backgrounds were much rarer and consequently more revered. There is still a small trust fund, though it is rumoured that from time to time, when His Highness goes into seclusion, he has actually found it necessary to disappear into the more shadowy sections of Old Montreal to wait on tables.

I am not sure where I heard this. It is the kind of information one receives by intuition. We would never speak of it publicly.

◇◇◇

I left Goa at the age of fifteen with one suitcase, a Parsi family name, a saint's Christian name (in Goa we are all named for the saint on whose day we were born), a history of family acrimony, and a Goan's happy nonchalance with it all. It is wise to acquire imperturbability with a name like Perpetua Engine-wallah. Anyway, I do not believe it is possible to grow up in the moist tropics without an instinctive and insouciant hedonism. It is quite possible to grow up in the *dry* tropics, in Mysore, say, or Hyderabad, or Allahabad, or Delhi, and be ascetic to the core. But those of us who drew childhood and adolescent breath on the dank monsoon side of the Western Ghats – whether we are Catholic, Parsi, Muslim, Syrian, Hindu, or Church of South India – know how to celebrate given bounty: of food, drink, ocean, beaches, the body.

So when I speak of family acrimony, I mean only this: the two halves of my family had no intercourse with each other, a state of affairs which is aberrant in India. My mother's family, Goan and Catholic, never acknowledged the existence of my father's family in Bombay. And vice versa. I think I recall that once our family priest told me that Zoroaster was the false prophet in the pit of hell who is referred to in the Book of

Revelation. Just the same, Father Diego and my father used to drink tea together on the verandah of the Queen Isabella, quoting Shakespeare interminably and competitively. Their tea was laced with brandy, and at about the time the sandalwood flares and mosquito coils were being lit, they would become somewhat more contentious, Father Diego reciting from *The Spiritual Exercises of St. Ignatius* and my father declaiming Persian and Urdu poetry in a caramel voice rich with vibrato.

My father taught English literature at San Miguel College (which shows how tolerant the Goan religious orders had become) until he gave a paper on "Zoroastrian Intimations in Marlowe's *Tamburlaine the Great*" at an international conference in Delhi. After this he received an invitation to teach at a prairie university in Canada and went. My mother refused to accompany him.

◇◇◇

It is now forty minutes after the hour designated as starting time on the *Diwali* invitations and we are probably drawing close to a beginning. Talk is muted. Children wander up and down the aisles in their new clothes, chattering to one another in English, a jasmine chain of fresh young faces. A tuning discourse is still going on between the sitar player and the tabla player, but they are beginning to nod their heads and smile and murmur *achaa, achaa* to each other.

They are sitting on a low platform, about the size of an overturned backyard sandbox, which has been placed on the stage and draped with Kashmiri rugs. The sitar player is barefoot and the tabla player is wearing black socks, one of which has a rather large hole at the heel. Both men are wearing dark Western trousers, loose cotton Punjabi tunics not tucked in, and Kashmiri vests, richly embroidered, that look oddly tiny over the ample tunics – like Day-Glo identifying colours daubed on the upper reaches of billowing sails. It is an eclectic mix that strikes me as being just right for the occasion.

Deftly the tabla player turns his drums and taps at the pegs with his little mallet. *Baap, baap*, the drums respond softly, like bleating oxen giving mournful answer when the cart driver twists their tails to force a little more speed over dusty roads. The copper *bayan*, which he plays with his left hand, pleases the tabla player. He bends over it, smiling, as though conferring a blessing, patting its skin gently – *pampetty pam pam* – with his fingers. And the sitar player answers, caressing his seven strings in congratulation. Oneness of pitch has been achieved.

But there is still a problem with the *dayan*, the drum for the right hand. It is made of wood and suffers from the dry air of central heating. *Baap, baap*, it says, faltering, sliding in and out of the desired pitch. The gourd of the sitar is also troubled by the dryness and two strings have strayed again. Tap, tap. Strum. Pegs turned, eyes closed, heads tilted sideways. I think of seagulls on the white sands of the Malabar coast, heads cocked into the wind, waiting, their patience endless.

It is a curious ritual, this. I wonder what the other Canadians would make of it, the ones who dispose of pre-concert tuning in a few hurried minutes as though it were something furtive and shameful. Of course this inability to perceive the wholeness of things is endemic to the Western mind. The very word foreplay, for instance. Suggesting a brief obligation to be got out of the way before the main event. They are strange people, Westerners.

But it is silly of me to say *they*. I feel *other* to Indians far more often. And I have learned to love Western music, I even have subscription tickets to the local symphony series, though there are things I will never get used to: that neurotic preoccupation with beginning on the dot of the advertised hour, coupled with the truly extraordinary custom of the blockade, of actually *barring entry* to anyone who arrives after the arbitrary moment in time when – in the opinion of an usher – a piece has officially begun. This is beyond comprehension. As is the puzzling absence of young children from concerts.

No sense of wholeness. That is what strikes me about the West. No awareness of the languid beauty of the tuning ceremony, of how it flows into the first *raga* whose sounds will curl into the ears and the veins of the little children like soft mists smoking up between the coconut palms when the monsoon pauses. And the mists will cling and the children will grow into the sounds and the memory of them, and the notes will flower into the gift of listening. And for some chosen few into the gift of creating new music.

Oh the lingering. The long soft scars left by music. I remember the concert my father took me to when I was four. It began at dusk and lasted most of the night and it comes back to me through all my senses: the sandalwood flares, the smell of musk and jasmine, the rustle of saris, the sounds of babies crying and children whispering and giggling, the soft shuffle of people arriving and leaving throughout the performance, the feel of my father's shoulder when my head finally sank there in sleep. Everything. For a *raga* cannot be separate from the hour of its playing or the sounds of its setting.

The *dayan* has reached agreement with its brother drum now. The players make *namaste* to the audience, parents gather their children onto their laps. The sitar player, who has been brought from Montreal for this occasion, chants a brief invocation and announces the *raga*. It flows around us. The radiators contribute metallic hiccups of expansion and occasional obbligatos of steam. Periodically the microphone (placed on the stage floor in front of the performance platform) speaks with a piercing electronic coloratura. Each time, someone in the front row gets up and fiddles with it and the soft magnified boom of his hand movements punctuates the *raga* like distant cannon.

We are dimly conscious of these separate details of sound. They are all part of the *raga* of an early winter evening in Canada, an unrepeatable performance, as each *raga* is.

For a short time I am able to exercise non-Indian skills of detachment and observation. I think of my seat at the local symphony concerts, seventh row centre. I recall the solemn hush, the decorum – a sacred rite that has come to excite me. For a short time I am able to look around and compare, to feel, even, briefly embarrassed. I note the rapt faces, the uncritical immersion in the spell, the eyes bright with tears, the full-scale Romantic-with-a-capital-R self-surrender. I am relieved that none of *the others* is present.

Across the aisle from me, His Highness is crying silently and unashamedly. Totally unselfconsciously.

And then I too enter the music, my ears full of jasmine petals, my eyes full of village festivals and tears.

◇◇◇

Much later, after the *Bharata Natyam* has been danced so charmingly by two of the teenage girls; after the university students have done their skit (a comic thing about the near-seduction of a young Canadian girl called Sita by a ne'er-do-well named Ravana, and about her rescue in the nick of time by Rama, a medical student chosen by her parents as a suitable match); after the paper plates and plastic forks and pot-luck curries, His Highness says to me, casually, and in the presence of several prominent citizens: "Miss Engine-wallah, I was speaking with your sister in Montreal last week. There's no need for you to go by train in the morning. I'm driving there on business tonight and I'm delighted to offer you a ride."

"Oh, Your Highness," I demur. "I wouldn't dream of putting you to such trouble."

His Highness draws himself up to his full six feet and two inches.

"I do not approve of a lady travelling alone on the train," he says. "I know it is very old-fashioned of me, but that is the way it is with our family. I would prefer that you travel under my protection."

His voice has the inflection of one used to authority.

"Perpetua," Mrs. Gopalan says, urging propriety. "I do think His Highness is right."

His Highness coughs. "With the support of Mrs. Gopalan," he says, "I insist."

"Your Highness is too kind," I murmur.

His Highness winks at me, ever so slightly, over the heads

of several people. Though of course it could have been merely an involuntary twitch of his eyelid.

❖❖❖

In the car we do not trouble to talk for a long time. Snow scuds across the road and catapults itself at the windshield in demented wraiths, a dance of Tantric devotees – though they also seem strangely like threshers flailing at the rice in the sun-white courtyards of Goa. His Highness, perhaps, sees the veiled women of the *zenana* dancing for his private pleasure. *Diwali* always lets us loose into our separate pasts.

I am pondering also the usefulness of my sister – though she is not my sister really, and she lives in Saskatoon. After my mother died of a perfectly standard tropical fever, I wrote to my father and told him I wanted to come to Canada. I had not seen him for six years, and it took a dozen letters back and forth to cajole him into sending for me. What no one knew, not even my Bombay grandparents, and what my father had neglected to mention in the annual letters he sent me on my birthdays, was that he had quietly remarried, and had two stepbrothers and a half-sister as well as a stepmother waiting for me. He met me at the airport in Saskatoon and explained all this. He said he thought it better not to upset anyone back home by telling them.

I must have looked subdued.

He put his arm around me. "You're old enough to understand that these things happen," he said. "And for a Parsi, education is the main thing. In Canada the very best is possible."

My stepmother was an Italian who had been widowed. My father was definitely attracted to Catholics. It was linked, I think, to his love of Persian and Urdu poetry. He recognized that romantic tension between rigid prescriptive discipline and passionate intensity.

❖❖❖

His Highness has reserved a table for us at Le Château Champlain, the same table as last year. I am always touched by this extravagance since it is almost certain he has to pay for it by considerable bartending in brasseries far inferior to this. (Of course a ritzy place like Le Château Champlain would offer anything to have such a princely *maître d'* but His Highness cannot work where he might be seen by any of us. It would be an unthinkable shame for everyone.)

"Prince Sana'ullah," I begin, ritually.

"Please," he says, as always. "You must call me Sani. I insist. We set no store by titles in my family. The throne, I can assure you" – he assures me – "is a very lonely place."

"It is difficult, Your Highness, to be so familiar –"

"You must try, Perpetua. To please me."

"I don't know how to thank you, Your Highness ... Sani, for such a beautiful evening."

"There is a full moon," he says. "Did you notice? The way it poured gold on the snow, the way the bare trees looked against it. I thought of how the minarets looked against the moon."

He lapses into silence, hearing a *muezzin* call perhaps.

"In Goa," I say, "when there's a full moon, it's bright as day." I remember how it was: the white sands and white buildings glistening, and the palms waving like dark bunches of ribbons.

"Did you ever see the Taj by moonlight?" His Highness asks.

"I've never seen the Taj. I flew from Goa to Bombay and then to Montreal and Saskatoon. I've never been back."

He winces as though I have punctured something, or have read from the wrong script. He seems disoriented. "Agra," he says, thinking aloud. "We all see Agra. It's required. I must have been ten. Just before being packed off to Eton the first time. Then back and forth, back and forth. Always back for the worst time, that hot dead time before the monsoon."

"There's been trouble near Agra," I say. "Did you see in the *Times*?" (I mean, by this, *The Times of India*. We all buy it from Mr. Motilal who has copies airmailed in to his news-agency.) "It seems Mrs. Gandhi –"

"Yes, yes," he says, brushing this aside. "It is inevitable.

I don't want to beat the drum or hoist the flag too much, you know, but when my great-grandfather ruled there was none of this . . . this pettifogging disruption."

We are both silent for a long time, I sipping my wine and Prince Sani his Scotch. (The Prophet, he is in the habit of saying, forbade only the fruit of the grape. On the subject of Scotch and cognac, he was silent.)

Our waiter comes and asks: *"Monsieur est prêt à commander maintenant?"* He has assumed from the start that we are French-speaking. Perhaps we have a Gallic aura of romance about us. We look, I suppose, exotic. Certainly not *des maudits Anglais.* ("This is a bilingual country," my father said. "And my children will be bilingual. Even in Saskatoon." In fact, of course, I became trilingual.)

His Highness says: *"Nous avons déjà mangé. Nous ne sommes ici que pour le dessert. Montrez-nous les pâtisseries, s'il vous plaît."*

His Highness learned his French at Eton, but his accent is pure *joual,* perfected in the sleazier taverns of Old Montreal. The waiter is nonplussed. He does not know what to make of the combination of aristocratic bearing, Parisian syntax, and Québécois street French. His Highness is indifferent to what the waiter thinks. When it comes down to pure physical presence, Prince Sani can make any man quail before the mere disdainful flutter of his royal eyelids.

After we have selected our pastries, he says to me gently: "It was a command, you know, what I said last year. I insist you do something about your future. I won't have you throwing your life away teaching school in a small stuffy town. It's such a waste. You're too beautiful and too intelligent."

"Thank you, Your Highness."

"Please, Perpetua. In my family we have never stood on ceremony. We do not hide behind our crown."

"Thank you, Sani."

"A private school in Montreal, at the very least. A modicum of elegance. The sisters will leap at the chance of having you."

"I've applied," I sigh. "All over. Nobody's leaping at the chance. Teaching jobs are hard to come by. I'm lucky to have the one I've got."

"It's not . . . *appropriate*," he sighs. "Also it's time for marriage. I ordered you to write to your family. Bombay and Goa, both."

"I did, Sani. My mother's family has arranged a match. I'm going back to Goa in July to be married."

"Back to Goa?" He is startled, as though a figure in his dream turned and tampered with his pillow.

"Just for the wedding. He's a professional man. Wants to emigrate to Canada. I've seen a photograph. And our horoscopes match."

"Well," he says. "That is very fine. Congratulations, Perpetua. It is the best thing."

We both think it probably is, given everything. Certain traditions are comforting in their way. It makes no sense to flout them. Pointless as railing at the monsoon. Nevertheless we lapse back into silence for a long time.

Finally I ask: "What about you, Sani?"

"My father also is arranging something. Negotiating with the girl's family. I think it will work out."

We stare at each other.

We are aware, suddenly, that this will be the last such *Diwali*. Not that the festival belongs to either of us; it is alien to both our traditions. In a sense. Except that it was part of the totality of our childhoods and it has this private significance: we met at the *Diwali* festival in our small town four years ago.

"You remember," His Highness says dreamily, "how the Taj looks in the moonlight?"

I smile fondly, beginning to believe I have seen it. For now the love-making has begun in earnest. Though of course it had already begun in the cloakroom before the concert, and was well under way when His Highness bowed to me across the aisle. It flows on through the murmur of nostalgia, the first accidental brushing of fingertips against fingertips, the holding of hands. It wafts us up to our reserved suite and through the long perfumed night while our bodies converse. They are attuned to each other, the *raga* they make is like the dialogue between sitar and tabla. Our love-making is present also in the intervals of talking and reverie.

Near dawn, His Highness sits up and greets the first light with Urdu poetry. His voice rises and falls, a musk of sound, a long ululating chant that curls into the niches of elsewhere. And that is when I begin to cry, helplessly and unstoppably. His Highness turns tactfully away, not because he is embarrassed, but because he does not want to intrude. He stands in the window and watches the neon strings of light along rue de la Gauchetière. He knows I have fallen into my childhood – my father and Father Diego on the verandah, my mother in the kitchen.

Once – I must have been about eight years old – my father took me to see San Sebastian, a splendid crumbling ruin of a Portuguese mission, still ghostly white in patches between the creepers. The jungle had reclaimed it, and peacocks screeched in its bell towers. But inside, where bats and monkeys made their home, we could still see the faintest old gold sheen of the saints fading into the walls and my father murmured: "*Sic transit gloria.* But remember this, Perpetua, it is only when glory has gone that it is appreciated. Do you think the ancient Persians were anything but military louts at the height of their imperial powers? It is now, in the twilight of Zoroaster, that our poetry and art enshrine them. Remember that, Perpetua. We love best what we have lost forever."

Prince Sani, naked and golden against the haze of city neon, turns away from the window.

I think about the fact that next summer Father Diego will unite me in matrimony with a man I have not yet seen. I wonder if he would consent to perform the ceremony in the ruined mission church?

His Highness takes me in his arms and brushes my damp cheeks with his silk handkerchief.

"Happy *Diwali*," he says, kissing me.

YOU GAVE ME HYACINTHS

S UMMER COMES HOT AND STEAMY with the heavy smell of raw sugar to the north-east coast of Australia. The cane pushes through the rotting window blinds and grows into the cracks and corners of the mind. It ripens in the heart at night, and its crushed sweetness drips into dreams. I have woken brushing from my eyelids the silky plumes that burst up into harvest time. And I have stood smoke-blackened as the cane fires licked the night sky, and kicked my way through the charred stubble after the men have slashed at the naked stalks and sent them churning through the mill. I have walked forever through the honeyed morning air to the crumbling high school – brave outpost of another civilization.

The class always seemed to be on the point of bulging out the windows. If I shut my eyes and thought hard I could probably remember all the faces and put a name to each. One never forgets that first year out of teachers' college, the first school, the first students. Dellis comes before anyone else, of course, feline and demanding, blotting out the others; Dellis, who sat stonily bored through classes and never turned in homework and wrote nothing at all on test papers. "Can't understand poetry," she said by way of explanation. There were detentions and earnest talks. At least, I was earnest; Dellis was bored. She put her case simply: "I'll fail everything anyway."

"But you don't *need* to, Dellis. It's a matter of your attitude, not your ability. What sort of job will you get if you don't finish high school?"

"Valesi's store. Or the kitchen at the mill canteen."

"Yes, well. But they will be very monotonous jobs, don't you think? Very boring."

"Yes." Flicking back the long blonde hair.

"Now just supposing you finished high school. Then what would you do?"

"Same thing. Work at Valesi's or in the mill canteen. Till I'm married. Everybody does."

"You could go to Brisbane, or even Sydney or Melbourne. There are any number of jobs you could get there if you were to finish high school. There would be theatres to go to, plays to see. And libraries. Dellis, this town doesn't even have a library."

Silence.

"Have you ever been out of this town, Dellis?"

"Been to Cairns once."

Cairns. Twenty thousand people, and less than a hundred miles away: the local idea of the Big City.

"Dellis, what are you going to do with your life?"

No answer.

I felt angry, as though I were the one trapped in the slow rhythm of a small tropical town. "Can you possibly be content," I asked viciously, "to work at the mill, get married, have babies, and grow old in this shrivelled-up sun-blasted village?"

She was mildly puzzled at my outburst, but shrugged it off as being beyond her. "Reckon I'll have to marry the first boy who knocks me up," she said.

"You don't *have* to marry anybody, Dellis. No doubt you could fall in love with some boy in this town and be quite happy with him. But is that all you want?"

"Dunno. It's better'n *not* getting married."

I knew her parents were not around; perhaps they were dead; though more likely they were merely deserters who had found the lure of fruit picking in the south too rewarding to resist. I knew she lived with a married sister – the usual shabby wooden cottage with toddlers messily underfoot, everyone cowering away from the belligerent drunk who came home from the cane fields each night. The family, the town – it was an intolerable cocoon. She simply had to fight her way out of it, go south. I told her so. But her face was blank. The world beyond the town held neither fascination nor terror. I think she doubted the existence of anything beyond Cairns.

In the classroom the air was still and fetid. There was the stale sweat of forty students; there was also the sickly odour of molasses rolling in from the mill. An insistent wave of nausea lapped at me. Dellis's face seemed huge and close and glistened wetly the way all flesh did in the summer. She looked bored as always, though probably not so much at her detention as at the whole wearying business of an afternoon and evening still to be lived through – after which coolness would come for an hour or two, and even fitful sleep. Then another dank day would begin.

"Dellis, let's get out of here. Will you go for a walk with me?"

"Okay," she shrugged.

Outside the room things were immediately better. By itself, the molasses in the air was heavy and drowsy, but pleasant. We crunched down the drive and out the gate under the shade of the flame-trees.

"I love those," Dellis said, pointing upwards where the startling crimson flaunted itself against the sky.

"Why?"

She was suddenly angry. "Why? You always want to know why. You spoil things. I hate your classes. I hate poetry. It's stupid. Just sometimes there is a bit I like, but all you ever do is ask why. Why do I like it? And then I feel stupid because I never know why. I just like it, that's all. And you always spoil it."

We walked in silence the length of the street, which was the length of the town, past the post office, Cavallero's general store, Valesi's Snack Bar, and two pubs. The wind must have been blowing our way from the mill, because the soot settled on us gently as we walked. The men swilling their beer on the benches outside the pubs fell silent as we passed and their eyes felt uncomfortable on my damp skin. At the corner pub, someone called out "Hey, Dellis!" from the dark inside, and laughter fell into the dust as we rounded the corner and turned toward the mill.

Halfway between the corner and the mill, Dellis said suddenly, "I like the red. I had a red dress for the school dance, and naturally you know what they all said.... But the trees don't care. That's what I'd like to be. A flame-tree." We went on in silence again, having fallen into the mesmeric pattern of stepping from sleeper to sleeper of the narrow rail siding, until we came to the line of cane cars waiting outside the mill. Dellis reached into one and pulled out two short pieces. She handed one to me and started chewing the other.

"We really shouldn't, Dellis. It's stealing."

She eyed me sideways and shrugged. "You spoil things."

I tore off strips of bamboo-like skin with my teeth and sucked at the soft sweet fibres.

We had passed the mill, and were on the beach road. Two miles under that spiteful sun. Close to the cane there was some coolness, and we walked in the dusty three-foot strip between the road and the sugar plumes, sucking and chewing and spitting out the fibres. The dust came up in little puffs around our sandals. We said nothing, just chewed and spat. Only two cars passed us. The Howes all hung out of one and waved. The other was a pick-up truck headed for the mill.

About one and a half miles along, the narrow road suddenly emerged from its canyon of tall cane. A lot of cutting had been done, and a farmhouse stood alone in the shorn fields, white and blinding in the afternoon sun. The haze of colour around the front door was a profusion of Cooktown orchids, fragile waxen flowers, soft purple with a darker slash of purple at the heart. "Gian's house," said Dellis as we walked on, and into the cool cover of uncut cane again.

Gian! So that was why he always had an orchid to tuck brazenly behind one ear. He was seventeen years old, a Torres

Strait Islander: black, six feet tall, a purple flower nestled against his curly hair any time one saw him except in class. Gian, rakishly Polynesian, bending over that day after school till the impudent orchid and his incredible eyes were level with mine.

"Did you know that I killed my father, Miss?"

"Yes, Gian. I was told that when I first arrived."

"Well?" The eyes were incongruously blue, and watchful under the long silky lashes.

I knew the court verdict was self-defence, I knew his father had been blind drunk, a wife-beater on the rampage.

"Well?" Gian persisted.

I said lamely: "It must have been horrible."

"I hated him," Gian said without passion. "He was a bastard."

"I gather many people thought so."

"Well?"

"What are you asking me, Gian? How can I know what was the right thing to do? Only you can know that."

"I am the only person in this town who has killed a man. Do you realize that?"

We stared at each other, and then outrageously he let his eyes wander slowly down my body with blatant intent, and walked away. I was trembling. After that I was always afraid to look Gian in the eye, and he always dared me to. When I turned to write on the board, I could feel two burning spots on the back of my neck. And when I faced the class again, his eyes were waiting, and a slow grin would spread across his face. Yet it was not an insolent grin. That was what was most disturbing. It seemed to say that we two shared a daring and intimate secret. But he knew it and I didn't.

Dellis and I had reached the beach. It was deserted. We kicked off our sandals, lay down, and curled our toes into the warm sand. The palms cast a spindly shade that wasn't much help, but a tired wisp of sea breeze scuffled up the sand refreshingly from the calm water. So amazingly calm inside the reef. I never could get used to it. I had grown up with frenetic surf beaches, but from here you had to go a thousand miles down the coast before you got south of the Great Reef.

"Dellis, you must visit Brisbane this summer, and give yourself a swim in the surf for a Christmas present. You just can't imagine how exciting it is."

"Let's go swimming now. It's so bloody hot."

"But we don't have swimsuits."

"Just take our clothes off."

"But somebody might come."

Dellis stood up and unbuttoned her blouse. "You spoil things," she said. It hurt when she stood naked in front of me. She was only fifteen, and it wasn't fair. I almost told her how beautiful she was, but envy and embarrassment stopped me. This is her world, I thought; she is part of it, she belongs. She was tanned all over; there were no white parts. She ran down into the water without looking back.

I stood up and slipped off my dress, but then my heart failed me, and I went into the water with my underwear on. We must have swum for half an hour, and it was cool and pleasant. Then we ran along the water's edge for ten minutes or so to dry out. We dressed and lay on the sand again. "It's good to do that," Dellis murmured. "It's the best thing when you're unhappy."

"Are you often unhappy?"

The look she gave me suggested that if I had to ask such stupid questions, why did I call myself a teacher?

"What I meant, Dellis, is that I'd like to ... if you're unhappy, I would like to ... I mean, if there's any way I can help...."

"You don't even know how to chew cane properly." She was looking at me with a kind of affectionate contempt, as though I were an idiot child. "You don't know anything. You really don't know *anything*." She shook her head and grinned at me.

I smiled back. I wanted to tell her how much I was learning. I would have liked to speak of poetic symbols, and of the significance which flame-trees or Cooktown orchids would henceforth have for me. Instead I said: "Dellis, today.... Who would have thought? How could I have guessed, this morning, that today would be so ... would be such a ...? Well, a *remarkable* day."

"Really? Why?"

"You spoil things. Don't ask me why."

She giggled. "But really, why?"

"It's very complicated. It has a lot to do with a religious and sheltered background that you couldn't even begin to imagine, and it would take a lot of explaining. But to put it briefly, it is a truly extraordinary thing for me to have gone swimming naked with one of my students."

"You didn't even take all your clothes off," she laughed.

Now the silence was close and comfortable, and longer and drowsier. We must have dozed, because when I sat up again the humidity was even more oppressive and monstrous dark clouds had billowed up out of the sea.

"There's going to be a thunderstorm, Dellis. We'd better get home quickly."

"Too early in the year," she said sleepily. And when she saw the clouds, "It'll ruin a lot of cane."

We were walking quickly, and nearly at Gian's house again, when Dellis pointed into the shadowy green maze of the cane field and said, "That's where Gian and I did it."

"Did what?"

"*Did* it. He laid me."

"Oh!... I ... I see. Your first...?"

She looked at me, startled, and laughed. "He's the only one I loved. And the only one I wouldn't take money from."

Virgin and child in a field of green. No madonna could have beheld the amazing fruit of her womb with more awed astonishment than I felt. Something hurt at the back of my head, and I reached up vaguely with my hand. There was a whole ordered moral world there somewhere. But I couldn't find it. It wouldn't come.

I said, inanely: "So you and Gian are in love?"

"He was going to give me money and I wouldn't take it. But he was gentle. And afterwards he took the orchid from behind his ear and put it between my legs. I hoped I'd have a baby, but I didn't."

The storm was coming and we fled before the wind and the

rain. At the mill we separated, but Dellis ran back and grabbed my arm. She had to shout, and even then I thought I hadn't heard her properly. Our skirts bucked about our legs like wet sails, runnels of water sluiced over our ears. She shouted again: "Have you ever been laid?"

"Dellis!"

"Have you?"

"This is not ... this is not a proper...."

"Have you?"

"No."

"Gian says you're beautiful. Gian says that you.... He says he would like to.... That's why I hated you. But now I don't."

Then we ran for our lives.

All through my dinner and all through the evening, the rain drummed on the iron roof, and the wind dashed the banana palms against the window in a violent tattoo. For some reason I wanted to dance to the night's jazz rhythm. But then surely there was something more insistent than the thunder, a battering on my door. She was standing dripping wet on my doorstep.

"Dellis, for God's sake, what are you doing here? It's almost midnight."

"They were fighting at home again, and I couldn't stand it. I brought something for you."

She held out a very perfect Cooktown orchid. Somebody's prize bloom, stolen.

"Come inside, out of the rain," I said vaguely, listening to the lines from Eliot that fluted in my head – fragments and images half-remembered. I had to take down the book, so I showed her the passage:

> 'You gave me hyacinths first a year ago;
> 'They called me the hyacinth girl.'
> – Yet when we came back, late, from the Hyacinth garden,
> Your arms full, and your hair wet, I could not
> Speak, and my eyes failed, I was neither
> Living nor dead, and I knew nothing,
> Looking into the heart of light, the silence.

"Dellis," I said, as (teacherly, motherly) I combed out her wet tangled hair, "for me, you will always be the hyacinth girl."

"*Poetry!*" she sniffed. And then: "What do hyacinths look like?"

"I don't know. I imagine they look like Cooktown orchids."

THE INSIDE STORY

G ENUFLECTION CAN BE DISTURBING. I noticed the oddly sup-
pliant man when I signed in, his boot soles gawping at
the public while someone attended to his ankles. His knees were
crammed together on a stackaway chair, his locked hands rested
on its back. God damn you, you sons of bitches, he doubtless
prayed.

These things upset me. I was not at all suited to the job,
but I got by with endless inner dialogue and a lunatic devotion
to curriculum. After the sign-in, the identicheck, and the various
double doors, I asked my class: "Do they always hobble you
like that in public?"

What do you mean, in public? they demanded. This is an
exclusive place. You've got to belong to be here.

"It seems so ... so unnecessarily distressing. Surely hand-
cuffs are sufficient?"

It's not so bad, they said. Except for boarding buses. And
for dancing. It's a definite handicap at dances.

My class had a very stern rule about cheerfulness. I was
often reproached for transgressing it. We can't afford your
romantic empathy, they would say. Please check your *angst*
in at the cloakroom before you see us.

On the day of the hobbling I had brought the Malamud novel.
With *The Fixer* I hoped to broach barricades that had not bent
for *Ivan Denisovich*. Curriculum content was a sore point, but
nothing could be done about it. The budget would not run to

33

a new set of multiple orders and English 101 was blue chip currency with the parole board, not to be traded in lightly. They were stuck with me and my reading list.

"I thought you would enjoy the prisoner as hero," I protested.

Hero! they said witheringly. That whining little Denisonov-abitch! He's just your regular run-of-the-mill convict. He's a paperback hero here only because he's in Russia. We could tell you a few things that would make us heroes in Russia.

"I detect jealousy," I said. "You're jealous of Ivan Denisovich, and of Solzhenitsyn too. You want to be famous prisoners."

You are a very sassy broad, they said.

"Kierkegaard suggested that we are all equally despairing, but unless we can write and become famous for our despair, it is not worth the trouble to despair and show it."

You people with a tragic world view, they sighed, you make life so difficult for the rest of us.

❖❖❖

George came to the door. He came twice a day in his white coveralls with his pail and putty knife.

"Haven't you got any broken windows?" he would ask wistfully.

He had been doing this for ten years, and is undoubtedly still doing it. A long time ago he killed someone.

❖❖❖

Actually, the class did like the Fixer, solitary and unbowed.

"Tell me," I begged with indecent eagerness – I have a sort of prurient interest in the metaphysical underpinnings of others – "how is it possible to endure such brutality and deprivation? How does anyone survive that? How does he stay human?"

It is comparatively easy, they said, when you are *completely* alone. It is fairly simple when the guards treat you like a dog. The real danger, the greatest threat, is the friendly keeper.

"But the degrading body searches?" I pursued. "The invasion of the Fixer's physical self? How does anyone survive that?"

The body can adapt to anything, anything at all, they said.

Beating, hunger, cold, humiliation. We speak from experience. You would be surprised how simple it is to separate yourself from your body. But head space is another matter. There is no foolproof defence against the invasion of private head space. Ivan Denisovich had it easy. Just plain physical hardship, too exhausting for dreaming or thinking. The Fixer had it much worse, but at least he was alone. We are in graver danger than either of them. We have shrinks and counsellors and classification officers.

"It is not true that the body can adapt to anything at all," I said. "I will add Franz Fanon to your reading list. It is ludicrous for you to talk so glibly when you know nothing of torture or concentration camps or Siberian cold."

It is even more ludicrous, they said quietly (they forgave me many moments of rashness), for you who know nothing of either body invasion or head invasion to presume to judge which is worse. We will not read Fanon – although we've never heard of him but can guess he's another tragic bloody humanist – because that would be the kind of invasion of our head space we can't afford in here.

"But you see – you must see – it is terribly important to answer these questions. How can there be any hope for us if we don't have an ideal of moral survival like the Fixer's? I hear you talking about the 'sleaze.' I see the gestures you make. I know the men you all consider sleazes. You see, for you too, salvation lies in *not* being a sleaze."

Oh *salvation*! they said. It is not exactly a major concern here, lady.

"But it is, it is. Or at least damnation is. The sleaze is damned. But he's only someone who has cracked under pressure. And all of us must have a cracking point, given torture. I'm deeply ashamed of it, but I'm sure I'd break at the first instant of physical brutality. Or even before that, at the mere fear of it."

You are not allowing for the rage, they said. Because you've never experienced it, you can't conceive of the rage you would feel at physical abuse. There's a lot of energy there. It convinces you you're right. The Fixer, for example, could see that he was driving those pigs crazy. He had something they wanted so badly – the sight of him snivelling – that it was pure pleasure not to give it to them.

"I wish I could believe you, but surely fear is greater than rage."

Not yours, they said. You get so worked up about these things. A good sign, if you're hung up on salvation. You'd get mad as hell and it would jolt you right out of all that garbage of fear you carry around inside your skull. Besides, you can take it from us, and we are experts on this subject, you are not and never could be a sleaze.

No other award, I am embarrassed to confess, has comforted me so much.

◇◇◇

"Haven't you got any broken windows in here?" George asked from the door. "I fix them good."

He sighed.

"Just ain't nothing for a skilled craftsman to do these days."

◇◇◇

"You know," Jed said to me privately after class, "I don't mean to make an issue of it. It's no big thing. But we *do* know what torture is, we just don't give it such a fancy name. See, I was twelve when they had me up for B and E the first time. They were *interrogating* me, you know, licking their dirty lips. Three white cops staring at one naked black kid, scared shitless. Used a fireplace poker to jab me in the balls. You'd be amazed how many cops are perverted queers. But then, you wouldn't believe me. We're the guys your mother told you to stay away from. Nothing but grief, baby."

◇◇◇

One lunch-time, in the staff room, a guard asked me: "Have those snivelling S.O.B.s told you their cruddy little life stories yet? Every one a bleeding tragedy. They get better and better in the reruns. Mark my word, by the end of the term your whole class will be orphans with unhappy childhoods."

◇◇◇

"Another thing," Jed said to me. "Get the hell out of this job. What kind of a nut are you? You think because we like you you're safe. You're too hung up on heroics. That shit just don't mean anything to us. Listen hard now. To me personally, and to a lot of the guys here, you are the sunshine itself. And I would like to pretend that I would lay down my life etcetera for you. Listen, when they throw me in The Hole, I don't give an inch. If I were the Fixer, just me against the screws, I wouldn't crack. But if things were to blow up here – everyone *inside* against everyone *outside* – and you were in the middle of it, I couldn't promise you a thing. I can't tell you what I'd do. I don't even know. I've been through one riot inside and it scared the shit out of me. I saw some ugly things and I did some ugly things. I'll tell you something – people inside dread blow-ups more than the screws do. I'm telling you this so you won't take it personally if anything happens. But I would consider it a favour if you would get your luscious little ass out of here, because you are such a stupid innocent snowflake in this hothouse, you make me weep."

◇◇◇

Protoplasmic, was how I thought of the class. Fluid in shape and structure, observers drifting in and out to watch and listen, credit students being drafted out to yard work or to The Hole or to other penitentiaries, reappearing and disappearing.

I could have looked up records, separated the murderers and thugs from the embezzlers, but I never did. Better not to know. Occasionally fragments of inadvertent information would slip out, but students were generally reticent about their pasts.

One student was a proselytizing TM-er. If you have deep inner tranquillity, he said, you can make disciplined decisions even in times of chaos and crisis. For example, there had been a moment during his last bank robbery when he had a gun pointed at a policeman's head. In the frenzy of that instant he had had to weigh immediate getaway (which would have been possible had he pulled the trigger) against a lifetime of being wanted for a capital offence. If it were not for TM he would have blasted out in the heat of the moment. As it was, he had only a six-year sentence.

"Armed bank robbery!" I was astonished. He was slight and dreaming, with the mystic's eyes of intense vacancy.

"I was charged with six armed robberies."

"Six!"

"They only have evidence for one," he said modestly, "and they wouldn't have got that without plea bargaining. I am a very careful planner. I hate violence."

Zen and the art of, I thought.

◇◇◇

George came to the door again.

"Haven't you . . . ?" he asked sadly.

Oh George, they said, we'd gladly break a window for you. Only it would mean The Hole, you know. Which of course we love – all that privacy and special attention. But we mustn't be selfish. Been there a lot lately. Got to give someone else a turn.

"I fix them good," said George. "I'm a real craftsman. Well, let me know . . ."

◇◇◇

Christmas was a bad time. During the preceding weeks, a guard came to the classroom door with the day passes, just two or three each day to keep up the air of seasonal expectation. The class was monumentally indifferent. What a bore, they said, when their names were not called. Look at all the snow beyond these cozy walls! Who wants pneumonia for Christmas! No one to cook your meals, no one to see that you're safely tucked in for the night. New Year's re-entry hangover, who wants it?

Joe's eyes always slithered away from official visitors in bored disdain. And just before Christmas, the giver of gifts smiled upon him. Joe stared back.

"None for you, shithead," said the guard. "You don't think they'd let an animal like you loose at Christmas, do you?"

Joe's fist hit the desk like a jackhammer on bedrock. Get out of here, you asshole! he blazed, and spent Christmas in The Hole.

"I hate those Steve McQueen movies," said the bank robber who meditated. "Very irresponsible. They give young kids the idea that bank robbing is glamorous, just a joy-ride. It is not glamorous, it is hard and bitter work. I may have started young, but I can honestly say" – he said it with moral fervour – "that I never once did it for kicks. I only did it for the money."

"I have a favour to ask you," said Jed.

I had been dreading this, being asked to carry out letters or bring something in. But it wasn't that. I must have been lucky. They never inflicted that decision on me.

"It's about Joe," he said. "You know how he is. From cold start to karate in one second flat."

I had noticed this. You should figure out some intermediate steps for anger, I told him. Try grinding your teeth and clenching your fists first. It burns up some of the energy.

That was after the episode of his chivalry. One of the drifters – those people not taking the course for credit but assigned to the school wing for some vague reason or other – had interrupted the class with a lewd joke. Joe had smiled softly and beckoned the drifter out of the room. He returned alone a few minutes later.

"I gave him a little tap on the head," he told me. "He'll sleep it off in an hour or so. He shouldn't have been disrespectful to you."

"Joe's a good man," said Jed. "But they have it in for him here because he assaulted a cop. I'm telling you this because he's up for parole again and he has to stay cool. They keep turning him down. He hasn't even been out on a day pass in five years. I'm just asking you as a special favour to avoid any mention of politics, philosophy, civil rights for queers, that kind of stuff, for a couple of weeks. Don't stir up his head space, you know? He has to stay cool."

I promised. We had a quiet week. No word. No word. Joe skittish as an unbroken colt and still no word from his classification officer. At the end of a week, right in the middle of a discussion of Kafka's *Castle*, he suddenly stood up and bellowed. Like a gored bull.

And then he said in a quite normal voice: "It's better to blow it and be done with it."

He blew it with style and with furious fist in the face of the guard who always said, "Keep your eyes off the lady there, you scum."

It must have been satisfying.

"At least I was in control," Joe told me after his spell in The Hole. "I didn't wait sweating and grovelling for them."

❖❖❖

"Why do you come here, anyway?" my class asked.

"No choice. We tragic bloody humanists have problems with our esoteric educations, you see. At the moment my skills are about as useful in the job market as fluency in Latin."

"You mean you're just doing it for the money?"

"That's right."

"Well, thank God. We were always afraid you had some goddamn *humanitarian* reason. Those kind of people make us nervous, you know?"

❖❖❖

"Why do you stay?" I asked a guard, one of the few who spoke with the enemy. (Me, that is. And the padres and such.) He had signed up, he said, when they were recruiting for a "better type" with college degree and idealism and compassion. What a laugh. The institution could only operate in black and white, he said. Grey got it from both sides. Get out, he said, while you're still human. Don't blame the staff for hating your guts though. You're a real threat. You get taken hostage, it's our lives on the line too.

"But why do *you* stay?"

"I stay because ten years in the Penitentiary Service does nothing for a résumé. This isn't exactly a stepping stone to an executive career. I stay because at least it's an income."

✧✧✧

"Why do you do it?" asked another staffer bitterly. "You think you can reform them with culture? Or you just get your kicks out of making it with a hood?"

"I need the money," I said. "Can't get anything else."

"Yeah?" he said, more kindly. "It burns me up, those shits getting a college education for free while I bust my guts and risk my life so that *maybe* my son can have one though his pa never did."

✧✧✧

"Why do you do it?" asked my chiropractor.

"I do it so I can pay your bills."

"If you quit that job," he said, kneading the snarled nerves and muscles in my back and neck, "you wouldn't need me."

✧✧✧

Ultimately the decision was taken out of my hands. Couldn't sign in. Emergency conditions, they said at the desk. No one admitted until further notice.

"How much further?"

"Months probably."

"What happened?"

"A stabbing, followed by the usual pandemonium."

I read the details in the evening paper. It was Jed, killed by Joe. Nothing but grief, baby.

✧✧✧

About six months later, I met a member of my class, out on parole.

"Poor dumb Joe," he said. "He never meant to hurt Jed, of all people. You know how he was. They say he's been really weird ever since. Of course he was transferred right out to Maximum, but we get news. They say you wouldn't recognize him. Shuffles around like a sad elephant. Smiles all the time, like old George. You remember old George, the window fixer? They say Joe's like that. Except for when he gets mad again, of course."

"What happened?"

"Joe got this letter, see, from his old lady. She's going to have a baby and of course Joe hasn't been outside for years. (Stupid dumb broad, why does she have to tell him?) Jed is going around telling everyone to give Joe space, give him time, let him be cool. And we're in the showers, see, and we can actually hear Joe sobbing. At first everyone thinks it's just the sound of the showers, but it has a different sound and it gets louder. Well everyone is minding his own business, and Joe is facing the wall close up to the shower, and Jed is giving everyone the hard look just in case, but then gradually the showers are turning off and Joe is consequently sounding louder. So I think Jed is planning to turn more showers back on, because he steps across near Joe and Joe just turns and bellows and stabs. Christ it was a mess with the showers and steam and fountains of blood and all.

"You know," he said. "The guys would like it if you'd write once in a while. Especially Joe probably. He always liked you, Joe did."

◇◇◇

I would like to stop feeling guilty about never having written to Joe, or anyone inside. I should never have taken that job. At least, thank God, as Jed sometimes used to remind the class, I was only doing it for the money.

MOVING OUT

THE DAY THE SOLD STICKER was pasted over the sign on the Hamiltons' front lawn, Mrs. Phillips realized what good neighbours they had been. The sticker and its iridescently orange four-letter word were askew, slanting downhill (everything would be downhill now, probably), dribbling gluey water across the realty company's logo. What she was reminded of, suddenly and incongruously, was the sort of unwelcome wet kiss imprecisely smeared across the cheek by senile relatives.

So it had really happened. What possible reason could the Hamiltons have for moving? Of course she would never ask. For a month the FOR SALE sign had been on the lawn but she had simply discounted its reality. True, on the first day she had stared at it as though it were perhaps a pig with wings which had fluttered down on the lawn, but days had gone by and nothing had happened. She and the Hamiltons had exchanged good mornings as usual while picking up their newspapers from their front porches. No one mentioned the sign. Mrs. Phillips had brushed it from her mind as one does the absurdities of nightmares on waking.

Sold.

Now that they were going she felt that she would certainly invite the Hamiltons in for afternoon tea and seed-cake. She had been toying with the idea for a year or so, considering the proprieties, weighing costs and benefits. Such an overture would certainly have been quite inappropriate any earlier than the blizzard of two winters back. After the blizzard new dimensions of neighbourliness had become possible, although one had to be careful never to rush things.

The blizzard had brought Mr. Hamilton to her very door, blinking the crust of icicles from his lashes, struggling through the whiplash of white that funnelled down between their houses, pulling his way through the drifts by means of a rope he had thrown across to her porch. She had heard the thud of the grappling hook and had thought: the tree has gone. But it had been Mr. Hamilton.

Did she need any firewood? Any dried milk? Any flour or yeast? Of course she had a safe supply of all these things. She had lived through her share of bad winters. She did not take chances. But she had been deeply moved by his concern, had invited him in for hot tea before he made the return journey. He had thanked her and declined, heading straight back to Mrs. Hamilton who was under ambush from arthritis.

They had never been inside one another's houses, though it had come close to that as the blizzard lashed its tail across the tenth day. It had come close to that for all of them, for the Cotters on her north side and for Mrs. Watts across the street. It had almost come to pooling firewood and oil and all moving into just one of their houses (whose would they have chosen?). But the police and the army had made the rounds with snowmobiles and emergency supplies before such an alarming experiment had become necessary.

Afterwards there had been a different feeling among them all, a certain confidence of kinship, not to be abused or taken advantage of, but definitely there. Any time since the blizzard it would probably have been possible to invite the neighbours in if she could have thought of the proper way to go about it. She did not want to be crass and forward and *organizing* in the manner of all these new professional youngsters – doctors and lawyers and college professors – who were filling up the city like so many dandelions taking over a flawless lawn; young people who insisted on referring to the city as "the town"; who flitted off to Toronto and Montreal on weekends like seed puffs to a weed patch; who held incessant dinner parties where one was required to make conversation with people one had no particular desire to meet.

No. She did not want to impose herself. She had to be careful. She was a newcomer herself. It was scarcely six years since she had bought the house.

A newcomer and not a newcomer.

She belonged. She understood what was expected. She had been born in a house just a few blocks away. From her upstairs window she could see the school she had attended. But then she had gone away to the great cities herself, had left for university and marriage and children and her life.

The children had grown up and set out on their own odysseys.

Widowhood had fallen greyly across her days like a shade pulled down by someone else's hand.

Life is circular, she thought, and decided to return to her roots. She used the insurance money to buy a rambling house in her own part of the city, the old ward of tree-lined streets, of limestone and brick houses, of gables and turrets and gracefully corniced doorways. It was the right sort of city in which to be a widow.

"Good grief, Mother!" protested her son who was a banker close to the pulses of power. Her quaint ancestral urge irritated him. "What on earth do you want to rattle around in a vast house like that for? The maintenance will bankrupt you. If you must move so inconveniently far away from us, what you need is a condominium on the lake front. Or if you insist on history, one of those little stone cottages on lower Earl Street. That's much more suitable for a ... you know, for someone at your stage of life."

But Mrs. Phillips wanted graciousness and privacy. She did not want to share her stairwell with other people or to own only one side of a wall. She wanted a garden big enough for lilacs and a crab apple, with a little stone path between rose bushes. She wanted the right sort of living-room for her harpsichord.

"Well," her son conceded huffily, "you can always take in

student boarders on the top floor, I suppose. Fortunately you're walking distance from the university, and location is the name of that game, you know."

"Oh yes," she said mildly.

Her son's work had much to do with games and gambits. She had always felt that this sort of thing was best left to the men of the family. They invariably worked something out; or rather, perhaps, matters of property and finance invariably worked themselves out. It was really a little vulgar to speak of such details even in the family, though these days, heaven knew, there were people who spoke as casually about money as they did about sex. Mrs. Phillips was glad to set a hedge of bridal wreath between herself and such discourse.

The SOLD sticker leered at her like a lapse in decorum.

Perhaps the new neighbours would be a young assistant professor with a wife and small children. The wife would undoubtedly be doing a master's degree in something or other and would be an aggressive conversationalist and an insistent inviter-in of neighbours. They would be the kind of people who believed in the triumphant public articulation of certain anatomical words. Penis, vagina, penis, vagina, their playful toddlers would chant to approving parental smiles. Mrs. Phillips had known the type in the big cities. She had hoped to escape them. She herself failed to see any intrinsic merit in calling a garden tool a spade.

But it might be much worse than that. The house might become a rabbit warren for students, with a landlord cramming bodies into every loophole in the zoning by-laws.

Mrs. Phillips had to sit down.

In the past year the houses on either side of Mrs. Watts, who lived opposite, had been converted. It was as though a rowdy motor cycle had ripped through the still life of the neighbourhood, spattering it with mud.

Mrs. Phillips' son said that property conversions in the area were a clear trend. It meant, he said, that his mother would get a good return on the house ("You sly old lady," he said), but there would be an optimal time to sell before the neighbourhood slid into irreversible decline. It meant, he said, that she should reconsider the condominiums by the lake.

It meant, Mrs. Phillips did not attempt to explain, that homes with history and lineage were being turned into three-storey filing cabinets for young bodies, that spacious rooms were being mutilated with partitions, and high ceilings defiled with fibreboard tiles bulk-ordered from the Sears catalogue.

It meant that enough was enough.

"What exactly do you have against the condominiums?" her son had asked.

"There are no mouldings around the door-frames."

"That is a frivolous reason," her son said, to which she had no answer.

"If it's peace and privacy you want, you'll have less and less of it here," he pointed out.

It was true. All summer the weekend tranquillity had been desiccated by student parties, the streets untidy with Frisbees and footballs and young men and women wearing suntans and fragments of clothing.

Everyone's front lawn and bushes had suffered. Mrs. Watts had done a lot of shouting and waving her cane; Mr. and Mrs. Cotter had sat in canvas chairs on their front porch, watching and sighing; but Mrs. Phillips, who was a little distressed by all that dazzling flesh, had responded by leaving the storm windows on even through the hottest weeks to blunt the noise. She had retreated to her living-room and her harpsichord. Once a football, horribly poised for several seconds, had stared at her through the double glass as though astounded by the tonal arrangements of Telemann. Mrs. Phillips had played diligently on through the discordant fracturing of her forsythia.

The SOLD sign appeared to her now as a score-board prophesying a siege of football games. She turned away from it and went to her writing desk. On her own embossed stationery she penned warmly worded little notes of invitation and delivered them herself to the Hamiltons, who were leaving; to the Cotters on her northern side; and to Mrs. Watts who had said often enough that the only way she would leave the house opposite was in a box.

◇◇◇

"We should have done this years ago," said Ada Watts, easing herself down between her canes. The sofa received her body, following the last few unexpectedly rapid inches of descent, with a soft slurp of surprise. "It takes a crisis. That's what my Harold used to say."

"Your Winston," corrected Mrs. Cotter.

"My what?" Ada Watts cupped her ear toward the speaker.

"Your Winston," Mrs. Cotter repeated, cranking her voice up a few notches. "Harold was your brother."

"Both of them," said Ada Watts with dignity. After fifteen years of widowhood, the confusion seemed to her irrelevant. A petty point. The kind Bessie Cotter had never been known to let slip. "Both of them used to say it. My Harold and my Winston. It takes a crisis."

"In the midst of life . . ." said Mr. Cotter sombrely.

There was a silence.

"Well, of course, people have a right to their privacy" – Ada Watts was looking pointedly at the Hamiltons – "but I always say, if you can't confide in your friends. . . ." Ada Watts came from a family which had lived in the town for generations; consequently she never needed to bother herself about other people's rules. She wore tweeds, though the last of her horses had been sold years ago, before Harold or Winston or whoever had died. She hitched one leg up over the other with casual inelegance to expose a large fish-pale bulge of thigh above her garter. Mrs. Phillips looked away quickly; Arthur Cotter stared with undisguised interest.

"I never pry into other folks' business." Mrs. Watts' thigh, coming to an arrangement with the sofa, stressed her point.

"Nobody *wants* to move, we all know that," Bessie Cotter offered helpfully.

The Hamiltons knew they were under siege; that *reasons* were called for.

"It was the wife's parents, you see." Jack Hamilton cleared his throat. "First her father last Easter, and now her mother's gone. Left us their house up country, you know. Huge place, family antiques, death duties, taxes, you know...." He spoke in a rush. "Had to sell one of the properties."

Well of course the others knew ... a death in the family, something like that.

The Hamiltons, naturally, had investigated the possibility of selling the country house instead, but there was the problem of moving the furniture. "Very expensive, you see," Jack Hamilton said. "We inquired. Believe me, we inquired. And then again it just didn't seem to fit here. Belongs in the other house, if you know what I mean."

"Oh well, in that case. Yes, yes, of course. Can't be helped." Ada Watts was unexpectedly onside, catching the sofa off guard. It made a sucking noise between her legs. "I tell my boys: those Queen Annes get moved from here over my dead body and you can tell your prissy wives: don't think I won't know, when I'm gone. The Queen Annes stay. As long as the house does."

The Hamiltons, with a surge of relief and warmth, spoke of how greatly they would miss the neighbourhood; and Bessie Cotter, sorrowful, commented on the improbability of a new owner looking after the rhubarb properly. Yes, the Hamiltons sighed. Leaving the garden was the worst.

"It takes a crisis. As my Harold used to say."

"Your Winston."

"Eh?"

"Your Winston. Harold was your brother."

"If Harold and Winston were here, they'd keep an eye on the rhubarb."

Bessie Cotter announced with a hint of tartness: "Mr. Cotter will keep an eye on it, won't you, Arthur? Remember how you used to mow the Watts' lawn for them because Winston was always away with the horses?"

"I've known you since three weeks after Noah came out of the ark, Bessie Cotter, and you haven't changed one bit. Never could resist putting in your two cents' worth."

"She came out of the ark flashing those hams," said Arthur Cotter in a ruminative mumble, thinking aloud. "Winston bait. Poor chap could never keep his eyes off her garters."

There was a stunned hush, followed by a gust of laughter from bare-thighed Ada Watts.

"It takes a crisis," she said. "We should have been doing this for years."

Yes, they all agreed. Yes. Such a good neighbourhood.

And who, Ada Watts wanted to know, were the buyers? Could they hope for kinfolk, or must they fortify themselves against a further siege of students?

No. Not students. An elderly couple.

An elderly couple! Wonderful!

"Anyone we know?"

The Hamiltons didn't think so.

"Moving here from somewhere else? Retiring?"

Yes, probably retiring. The Hamiltons were not sure.

"I'm so glad for the rhubarb. And your roses. Such a relief, only two people moving in. We were rather worried, you know, Arthur and I."

Well, actually ... more than two, perhaps. The agent had said something about a married son and a married daughter. . . .

"Good gracious! All in the same house? Very odd, isn't it?"

Yes, a bit unusual perhaps.

"University people?"

No. The Hamiltons thought not. A restaurant, they believed. Family business. Something like that.

Well, at least a family. Six people. It could have been so much worse.

Not six exactly, the Hamiltons confessed. The young couples had some children.

"How many children?"

Five in all, they believed.

Mrs. Phillips concentrated on her tea, swallowing hot sweet comfort. Ada Watts leaned forward and jabbed the air with one of her canes. "What is the name of these people?"

Mrs. Hamilton looked mournfully at her husband who looked at his hands. "We couldn't help it," he said apologetically. "We haven't even met them, you know. Agent arranged everything. Property taxes due on both places, you know. We had to have the money. They met our price. There was nothing we could do."

Mrs. Phillips proffered her teapot. "You mustn't think anyone is blaming you. These things happen."

The cane rapped out the question again: "What is the name?"

"The name is Wong."

"I knew it! I knew it!" Ada Watts gave a snort, part triumph at being undeceivable, part battle cry. "*The* Wongs, I suppose? Own half the real estate in town!"

Yes, the Hamiltons admitted forlornly. Those Wongs.

Ada Watts gyrated between her canes into an upright position. "First the Frisbees, now the soy sauce!" She stumped toward the front door and turned to admonish them all with one of her canes. "They'll tack on dormers and annexes, you know. They'll turn your house into a jigsaw puzzle. We won't see the block for boarders and parked cars." She pounded the hallway carpet with her cane. "They are trying to buy us all out, of course. First they'll drive us crazy, then they'll drive us out. Well, we shall see who gives in first! We shall see who the survivors are! Lovely seed-cake, Mrs. Phillips. We must do this again."

◇◇◇

The crocuses came and went, and then the moving vans, and then the lilacs. The summer annuals would last for months and so would the Frisbees and footballs. And so would the music. Forever, it seemed. If you could call it music. A cacophony of stereo decibels and drums and shrieking voices and bass vibrations that invaded the house even through the storm windows, setting the delicate nerves of the harpsichord on edge.

Of course, Mrs. Phillips reminded herself, with students it would have been exactly the same. Their kind of music. She simply had not had to deal with it stuttering up through the floorboards before, attacking the very ground she walked on. Thump, thump, vibrate. She would rather share her stairwell.

She spoke to the Cotters over the back fence as they both clipped off the last of the wilting peony blossoms and staked their tomatoes.

"I think I am going to buy a condominium after all."

"What's that you say?" Arthur Cotter asked, his hands full of mulch.

"A condominium. It's their radio. I simply cannot live with it. I've sealed up all the windows and I can shut out the *sound*, but I can still *feel* it."

"They're in our tomatoes too, you know. I've got something for it."

"No, no. The radio. I'm going to move, I think."

Arthur Cotter cupped his ear toward her. "Can't quite catch...."

"Says she's going," shouted Bessie Cotter. She explained: "Doesn't have his hearing aid on when he's gardening, you know." And shouted again: "She's going. She can't stand the Wongs."

"The what?"

"The Chinese family!" Bessie Cotter shouted into a sudden lull in the disc jockey's voice that boomed from the Wongs' kitchen window. "She can't stand them!"

"Oh no really!" Mrs. Phillips was dismayed, glancing over her shoulder. "They're very nice people, I'm sure. It's just their radio."

"The what?"

"Their radio!" she shouted.

"Radio doesn't bother us too much," Bessie Cotter said.

Deafness, thought Mrs. Phillips, has its advantages.

❖❖❖   •

Mrs. Phillips was unable to sleep. She understood why the music was called rock. She felt as though an avalanche of impermeable matter were pummelling her nerve ends. She got up and put on her robe, made herself some hot milk with cinnamon and honey, sat in her living-room and tried to think.

Around midnight, when everything was finally quiet, she tried the harpsichord. It had been jarred badly out of tune. She worked with silent absorption, tuning it. She began to play Vivaldi. She began to feel at peace. Life was manageable after all. One simply needed to make adjustments.

She heard a car swing into the neighbouring driveway, heard a babble of talk and laughter. The son and his wife were given to partying. Mrs. Phillips smiled benignly and played Vivaldi. To each his own life.

Then it came at her again, that intrusive insistent rhythm, that rude music. One o'clock in the morning. It was too much. She put her forehead against the keyboard and wept.

By dawn, after a tossing dream-riddled sleep, a solution had presented itself to her. She would simply visit her new neighbours and ask them very politely to turn their music down. A reasonable request, surely. People were rational. It was natural to want to get along with one's neighbours. There was no reason why they would refuse. Why was she shaking so? Why were her palms wet and cold?

After her second cup of coffee, she put on a light jacket and combed her hair. But her legs felt as though they were just testing themselves after a long illness and she had to sit down again. Too much coffee perhaps. She put on the kettle and made a pot of tea. She drank a cup.

Now, she told herself firmly, as she did on Sundays before visiting her aunt in the nursing home. This has to be done and that is all there is to it.

Outside it was clear and sunny and the Wongs' front path was a curious mosaic of mushrooms and roots spread on swathes of cheesecloth to dry in the sun. The old Mrs. Wong, a tiny figure, was sitting cross-legged beside the path, taking up one by one the gnarled root-like things, doing something to them with her fingers.

"Good morning," said Mrs. Phillips hesitantly, disconcerted by new irregularities.

The old lady looked at her and nodded several times.

"I wonder if I might have a word with your son perhaps? Or is it your son-in-law?"

The old lady nodded rapidly again and went on doing things to the roots.

"Ah, could you . . . could I? . . . Shall I go to your front door?"

She was wondering how to negotiate the mushrooms and reach the front steps without damaging anything. The old lady offered no suggestions. Mrs. Phillips tiptoed gingerly between the roots and reached the porch. There no longer seemed to be a doorbell, though a set of wind-chimes dangled down from the door-frame.

"Should I . . . do I tap the chimes?"

"No use talking to my mother," said a voice through the suddenly opened door. "She doesn't speak any English."

"Oh! Actually, it was you I wished to speak to, Mr. Wong. You are the son, I believe?"

"The son." He laughed loudly, in a high-pitched nasal way. "Yes indeed, ma'am. I am the son." His laugh sounded Chinese, but his voice sounded local. Home grown. And slightly snide. No different from her own son's. "What can I do for you?"

"I was wondering. . . ." She hated the way her voice quavered. "I have a small request. I don't like to make a fuss, but I wonder if you wouldn't mind playing your radio more softly, especially at night. Much more softly, actually."

He stared at her, his eyebrows puckering. "It's a free country, ma'am."

"Yes, of course it is. But we do . . . in this country, that is . . . we do try to respect each other's rights. We have very different tastes in music, you see. You people. . . ."

"What do you mean, *we people?*" he demanded belligerently.

"I mean: you people who like rock music. . . ."

"I was born in this country same as you, lady. You feel you have special privileges?"

"No, of course not, Mr. Wong. This is quite uncalled for. I

was only asking if it is necessary to have your radio quite so *loud*...."

"You been across the road to speak to those students about their stereos?"

"Well, no ... not yet ... because I keep my storm windows.... But if their sound carried ... if they kept me awake after midnight...."

"I've got more right than those students, lady. I've got legal title to this land and they're just tenants. My tenants, as it happens. Now if you'll excuse me."

He closed the door.

Mrs. Phillips felt decidedly unsteady. She leaned on the porch railing and sank down to sit on the top step. She put her hands to her cheeks and realized that she was weeping. It was not the sort of thing she approved of in public but she did not seem to be able to do anything about it.

I shall have to leave of course, she thought. The world of high ceilings and harpsichords and sweet neighbourhood silence was irretrievably lost. She had outlived it. It could not be transplanted to a condominium, it was as outmoded as gas lighting. Well, she had survived other losses.

She realized with embarrassment that old Mrs. Wong was staring at her.

"Oh, I'm so sorry. Crying here on your step. It's an upsetting time for me."

Then she remembered that Mrs. Wong did not speak English. What formidable isolation, she thought. How long has she been in this country? Thirty years, if the son was born here. At least thirty years.

"How have you been able to stand it?" she asked aloud. "Whom do you speak to? What have you lost?"

The old lady suddenly began to talk, earnestly, rapidly, in pell-mell Chinese. It seemed to Mrs. Phillips that she spoke of ancient courtyards and green rice paddies and granary floors. Of bound feet perhaps, and of family shrines.

Mrs. Phillips moved down to the bottom step. "Of course,"

she said, "as long as we are alive nothing is completely lost. In here and in here" – she touched her own forehead lightly, then Mrs. Wong's – "it is still complete." She formed a sphere with her hands. "Everything still exists whole for us."

Mrs. Wong nodded vehemently, smiling. She patted the ground beside her. Mrs. Phillips hesitated a moment. (She had never sat on the ground.) She kneeled instead, as though she were about to prune her roses, and began to help with the roots, breaking them into fragments with her fingers.

WAITING

MR. MATTHEW THOMAS owed his name and faith, as well as his lands, to those ancestors of lowly caste who had seen the salvation of the Lord. (It had been brought to South India by St. Thomas the Apostle, and by later waves of Portuguese Jesuits, Dutch Protestants, and British missionaries.) Now, heir of both East and West, Matthew Thomas sat quietly in one of the chairs at the crowded Air India office, waiting for his turn. It was necessary to make inquiries on behalf of a cousin of his wife, and although his wife had died ten years ago, these family obligations continued. The cousin, whose son was to be sent overseas for a brief period of foreign education, lived in the village of Parassala and could not get down to Trivandrum during the rice harvest. Mr. Matthew Thomas did not mind. He had much to think about on the subject of sons and daughters and foreign travel, and he was glad of this opportunity for quiet contemplation away from the noisy happiness of his son's house.

It was true that he had been waiting since nine o'clock that morning and it was now half past three in the afternoon. It was also true that things would have been more pleasant if the ceiling fan had been turning, for it was that steamy season when the monsoon is petering out, and the air hangs as still and hot and heavy as a mosquito net over a sick-bed. But the fan had limped to a halt over an hour ago, stricken by the almost daily power failure, and one simply accepted such little inconveniences.

Besides, Mr. Thomas could look from the comfortable vantage
point of today back toward yesterday, which had also been spent
at the Air India office, but since he had arrived too late to find
a chair it had been necessary to stand all day. At the end of
the day, someone had told him that he was supposed to sign
his name in the book at the desk and that he would be called
when his turn came. Wiser now, he had arrived early in the
morning, signed his name, and found a chair. He was confident
that his turn would come today, and until it did he could sit
and think in comfort. Mr. Thomas was often conscious of God's
goodness to him in such matters. All the gods were the same,
he reflected, thinking fondly of the auspicious match which had
just been arranged for the daughter of his neighbour Mr.
Balakrishnan Pillai. Lord Vishnu; Lord Shiva; the Allah of his
friend Mr. Karim, the baker; the One True God of his own
church: all protected their faithful. He did not dwell on paradox.
    God was merciful. It was sufficient.
    The problem which demanded attention, and which Mr.
Thomas turned over and over in his mind, peacefully and
appraisingly as he might examine one of his coconuts, concerned
both his married daughter in Burlington, Vermont, and the white
woman waiting in another chair in the Air India office.
    Burlingtonvermont. Burlingtonvermont. What a strange word
it was. This was how his son-in-law had pronounced it. His
daughter had explained in a letter that it was like saying
Trivandrum, Kerala. But who would ever say Trivandrum,
Kerala? Why would they say it? He had been deeply startled
yesterday morning to hear the word suddenly spoken aloud,
just when he was thinking of his daughter. Burlingtonvermont.
The white women had said it to the clerk at the counter, and
she had been told to write her name in the book and wait for
her turn.
    This is a strange and wonderful thing, he had thought. And
now he understood why God had arranged these two days of
waiting. It was ordained so that he would see this woman who
came, it seemed, from the place where his daughter was; so

that he might have time to study her at leisure and consider what he should do.

◇◇◇

He thought of Kumari, his youngest and favourite child. What did she do in Burlingtonvermont? He tried to picture her now that she was in her confinement, her silk sari swelling slightly over his grandchild. A terrible thought suddenly presented itself to him. If she had no servants, who was marketing for her at this time when she should not leave the house? Surely she herself was not...? No. His mind turned from the idea, yet the bothersome riddles accumulated.

She was in her third month now, so he knew from the four child-bearings of his own wife that she would be craving for sweet mango pickle. He had written to say he would send a package of this delicacy. *Dear daddy*, she had written back, *please do not send the sweet pickle. I have no need of anything. I am perfectly happy*.

How could this be? It was true that her parents-in-law lived only five kilometres distant in the same city, and her brother-in-law and his wife also lived close by, and of course they would do her marketing and bring her the foods she craved. Of course, they were her true family now that she was married. Even so, when a woman was in the family way, it was a time when she might return to the house of her father, when she would want to eat the delicacies of the house of her birth.

He could not complain of the marriage. He was very happy with the marriages of all four of his children. They had all made alliances with Christian families of high caste. He had been able to provide handsome dowries for his daughters, and the wives of his sons had brought both wealth and beauty with them. God had been good. It was just a little sad that his elder daughter's husband was chief government engineer for Tamil Nadu instead of Kerala, and was therefore living in Madras. But at least he saw them and his grandchildren at the annual festival of Onam.

It was four years since he had seen Kumari. The week after her wedding her husband and his family had returned to America, where they had been living for many years. Only to arrange the marriages of their sons had they come back to Kerala. The arrangements had been made through the mail. Mr. Thomas had been content because the family was distantly related on his wife's side and he had known them many years ago, before they had left for America. Also the son was a professor of chemistry at the university in Burlingtonvermont, which was fitting for his daughter who had her B.A. in English literature. So they had come, the wedding had taken place, and they had gone.

For four years Mr. Matthew Thomas had waited with increasing anxiety. What is a father to think when his daughter does not bear a child in all this time? Now, as God was merciful, a child was coming. Yet she had written: *Dear daddy, please do not send the sweet pickle. I am perfectly happy.*

It had been the same when he had expressed his shock at her not having servants. *Dear daddy*, she had written, *you do not understand. Here we are not needing servants. The machines are doing everything. Your daughter and your son-in-law are very happy.* Of course this was most reassuring, if only he could really believe it. He worried about the snow and the cold. How was it possible to live with such cold? He worried about the food. The food in America is terrible, some businessmen at the Secretariat had told him. It is having no flavour. In America, they are not using any chili peppers. And yet, even at such a time as this, she did not want the sweet pickle. Could it mean that she had changed, that she had become like a Western woman?

He looked steadily and intently at the white woman in the room. Certainly, he thought, my daughter will be one of the most beautiful women in America. White women were so unattractive. It was not just their wheat-coloured hair, which did indeed look strange, but they seemed to have no understanding of the proper methods of beauty. They let their hair fly as dry and fluffy as rice chaff at threshing time instead of combing it with coconut oil so that it hung wet and glossy.

The woman was wearing a sari, which was, without question, better than the other Western women he had sometimes seen at the Mascot Hotel; those women had worn trousers as if they were men. It was amazing that American men allowed their women to appear so ugly. True, he had heard it said that women in the north of India wore trousers, but Mr. Thomas did not believe it. An Indian woman would not do such a thing. Once he had seen a white woman in a short dress, of the kind worn by little girls, with half her legs brazenly showing. He had turned away in embarrassment.

Mr. Thomas was pleased that the woman from Burlington-vermont was wearing a sari. Still, it did not look right with pale skin and pale hair. It is the best she can do, he concluded to himself. It is simply not possible for them to look beautiful, no matter what they do.

The thing that was important, and must now be considered, was what to do with this manifestation sent by God. The woman from Burlingtonvermont perhaps had all the answers to his questions. Perhaps she could even explain the matter of the sweet pickle. But what to do? One did not speak to a woman outside of the family. And yet why else would it have been arranged that he should have two days to observe this very woman? God would also arrange the solution, he thought simply. He had only to wait.

As he continued to study that strange pale face an amazing thing happened. A tear rolled slowly down one cheek and fell into the soft folds of the sari. Mr. Thomas was shocked and looked away. After a little while, he looked back again. The woman seemed to be holding herself very tightly, as still as death, he thought. Her hands were clasped together in her lap so rigidly that the knuckles showed white. Her eyes were lowered, but the lashes glistened wetly. It must be a matter of love, he thought. Tragic love. Her parents have forbidden the match. For what other reason could a young woman, scarcely more than a girl, be weeping? Then his name was called and he went to the counter.

❖❖❖

At the counter, Mr. Chandrashekharan Nair consulted the timetables and folders which would answer the queries of Mr. Matthew Thomas. He handled his sheaves of printed information reverently, occasionally pausing to make a small notation in ink in one of the margins, or to dignify a page with one of his rubber stamps. It always gave him a sense of pleasurable power. It was so fitting that the Nairs, who had from ancient times guarded the Maharajah of Travancore and defended his lands, should be as it were the guardians of Kerala in this modern age, watchmen over all the means of entry and egress.

It had given him particular pleasure to announce the name of Mr. Matthew Thomas. It was like the pleasure which comes after a summer's day of torpid discomfort, when the air is as damp and still as funeral bindings, until the monsoon bursts in a torrent of cool blessing. Just such a salvific release from several days of tension had come when he passed over the name of Miss Jennifer Harper to announce instead that of Mr. Matthew Thomas.

Life was distressingly complicated at the moment for Chandrashekharan Nair, who was twenty-six years old, and who owed his present position to his master's degree in economics as well as to his uncle who was a regional manager for Air India. The trouble was that two years ago, when he was still a student at the University of Kerala, he had joined one of the Marxist student groups. Well, in a sense joined. They had been an interesting bunch, livelier than other students. Mostly low-caste of course, even Harijans, not the sort of people one usually associated with, and this gave a risqué sense of exhilaration. But the leaders had all been decent fellows from the right families – Nairs, Pillais, Iyers. They read a bit too much for his liking, but the demonstrations had been rather fun, milling along Mahatma Gandhi Road in front of the Secretariat, confusing the traffic, making the withered old buffalo-cart drivers curse, jeering at the occasional American tourist. It was a student sort of thing to do. He had not expected that they would hang on to him in this way. It was beginning to become very embarrassing.

Of course he was all for progress. He agreed that more had to be done for the poor people. He felt that when he had his own household he would not expect so much from the *peon* as his father did. They really should not make the boy walk five kilometres each noontime to take young Hari's lunch to him at college, he thought. It was too much for a twelve-year-old boy.

In theory, he also agreed with the Marxists about dowry. Nevertheless, when he had studied so hard for his master's degree, he felt he could expect a *lakh* of rupees from his bride's family. That was simple justice. He would be providing her with security and prestige. He had *earned* the money. Strictly speaking, it was not dowry. Dowries were illegal anyway. It was simply that a girl's family would be embarrassed not to provide well for her, and a bridegroom from a good family, with a master's degree into the bargain, had every right to expect that they provide for her in a manner suited to his status.

Chandrashekharan Nair's marriage, and his *lakh* of rupees, was all but arranged. There was one slight problem. The girl's family was raising questions about his associations with the Marxists. His father had assured them that this had been the passing fancy of a student, wild oats only, but they wanted something more, a public statement or action.

Chandrashekharan Nair was nervous. One of his cousins, who had held an influential position in the Congress party of Kerala, was now under attack in the newspapers. It was possible that he would have to stand trial for obscure things, and his career would be ruined. It did not seem likely that the Marxists would regain total power in Kerala, but they were becoming stronger all the time and one should not take chances. It was not wise to be on record for any political opinion, for or against anything. One should always appear knowing but vague, erudite but equivocal.

Chandrashekharan Nair leafed through the problems in his mind day after day as he leafed through the papers on his desk.

The girl's family was waiting. His own family was waiting. His father was becoming annoyed. It was simply not fair that he should be forced into such a dangerous position. Three days ago some of his former Marxist friends had come to the office. They were jubilant about the Coca-Cola business, and had just erected near the Secretariat a huge billboard showing Coca-Cola bottles toppling onto lots of little American businessmen who were scattering like ants. There was to be a major demonstration and they wanted him to take part.

All of Chandrashekharan Nair's anxiety became focused on the American girl who had walked into his office yesterday. It was her fault, the fault of Americans and their Coca-Cola and their independent women, that all these problems had come to plague his life. And then the glimmer of a solution appeared to him. He would make a public statement about Coca-Cola. He would praise the new Indian drink and the name chosen for it. He would mention Gandhi, he would say that this non-violent method, following in Gandhiji's footsteps, was the correct political way for India. All this was quite safe. Morarji Desai and Raj Narain were saying it in the newspapers every day. The girl's family would be satisfied. But he would also say a few carefully ambiguous words about American businessmen that would please the Marxists. And as he slid easily over Miss Jennifer Harper's name, he thought with a surge of delight of how he would tell his Marxist friends in private of his personal triumphant struggle with an imperialist in the Air India office.

He saw the tear run down Miss Jennifer Harper's cheek and frowned with disgust. He felt vindicated. Integrated. Both Hindu and Marxist teachings agreed: compassion and sentiment were signs of weakness. The West was indeed decadent.

◇◇◇

Jennifer Harper concentrated all her energy on waiting. There is just this one last ordeal, she promised herself, and even if I have to wait all tomorrow too, it must come to an end. I will not let the staring upset me. There is just this last time.

After months of conspicuous isolation as the only Western student at the University of Kerala, she was leaving. She wondered how long it would be before her sleep was free of hundreds of eyes staring the endless incurious stare of spectators at a circus. Or at a traffic accident. If one saw the bloodied remains of a total stranger spread across a road, one watched in just that way – with a fascinated absorption, yet removed, essentially unaffected.

She looked up at the counter with mute resignation. Surely her turn would come today. Inadvertently, she became aware of the intent gaze of the gentleman who had arrived next after her that morning. He also had waited all yesterday, but it did not seem to ruffle him. Nor did he show any sign of the exhausted dejection she had felt. Time means nothing to them, she thought with irritation. She decided to meet his gaze evenly, to stare him into submission.

He did not seem to notice. Her eyes bounced back off a stare as impenetrable as the packed red clay beneath the coconut palms. She felt as stupid and insignificant as a coconut, a stray green coconut that falls before its time, thuds onto the unyielding earth, and lies ignored, merely something for the scavenger dogs. It was intolerable. She could feel tears pricking her eyes.

Damn, damn, damn, she thought, pressing her hands together with all the force of her desire not to fall apart from the heat, the exhaustion, the dysentery, the inefficiency, the interminable waiting. Just this one last little thing, she pleaded with her self-respect. Then a name was called, and the impertinent staring gentleman went to the counter. They had missed her name by accident. But what would be the good of attempting to protest? Communication would be a shambles. The clerk would be confident that he was speaking English but would be virtually unintelligible. He would understand almost nothing she was trying to explain. Then she would try her halting Malayalam, but all her velar and palatal *r*s and *l*s, and all those impossible *d*s and *t*s, would get mixed up, and the people in the room would stare and giggle. Better to wait. He would soon notice that he had omitted a name.

◇◇◇

There was a blare of loudspeakers passing the office. No one paid any attention to it. Every day some demonstration or other muddled the already chaotic traffic of Trivandrum's main road. If it was not the Marxists, it would be the student unions of the Congress party or the Janata party marching to protest each other's corruptions. Or it would be the bus drivers on strike, or the teachers picketing the Secretariat, or the rubber workers clamouring for attention, or perhaps just a flower-strewn palanquin bearing the image of some guru or deity.

The blast from the loudspeaker was so close that those at the counter could not hear one another speak. There was a milling crowd at the Air India doors, which gave way suddenly to the pressure of bodies. Mr. Chandrashekharan Nair blanched to see several Marxist leaders. He was going to have to make some snap decision that might have frightening repercussions for the rest of his life. He breathed a prayer to Lord Vishnu.

Mr. Matthew Thomas, who knew that the ways of God were inscrutable but wise, felt that something important was about to happen and waited calmly for it.

Jennifer Harper thought with despair that the office would now be closed and she would have to come back again the next day.

The student leader made an impassioned speech in Malaya-lam, which culminated in a sweeping accusatory gesture toward Jennifer. She rose to her feet as if in the dock. The student advanced threateningly, glared, and said in heavily accented English: "Imperialists out of India!" In equally amateur Malaya-lam, and in a voice from which she was unable to keep a slight quiver, Jennifer replied, "But I am not an imperialist."

There was a wave of laughter, but whether it was directed at her accent or her politics she could not say. Several things happened so quickly that she could never quite remember the order afterward. First, she thought, the gentleman who had stared so hard stepped between herself and the student, pro-tective.

At the same time, the clerk at the desk had said, with a rather puzzling sense of importance, that he was especially arranging for the American woman to leave the country as quickly as possible. At any rate, she was now in a taxi on her way to the airport with nothing but her return ticket and her pocket-book. Next to the driver in the front seat was the gentleman who had defended her. She was thinking how sweet and easy and simple it was to sacrifice the few clothes and books, the purchased batiks and brasses, left back at the hostel. But the gentleman was saying something.

"My name is Matthew Thomas and I am having a daughter in Burlingtonvermont. I am hearing you say this place yesterday, and I am thinking perhaps you know my daughter?"

She shook her head and smiled.

"My daughter ... I am missing her very much.... She is having a child.... There are many things I am not understanding. ..."

They talked then, waiting at the airport where the fans were not working and the plane was late. When the boarding call finally came, Jennifer promised: "I will visit your daughter, and I will write. I understand all the things you want to know."

Mr. Matthew Thomas put his hands on her shoulders in a courteous formal embrace. She was startled and moved. "It is because you are the age of my daughter," he said, "and because you go to where she is."

Mr. Chandrashekharan Nair watched the plane circle overhead. He was on his way to the temple of Sree Padmanabha-swamy to receive prasadam and to give thanks to Lord Vishnu. He had just made a most satisfactory report of the incident to the newspaper reporter, and had been able to link it rather nicely to the Coca-Cola issue. It was a most auspicious day.

The ways of God are truly remarkable, thought Mr. Matthew Thomas as he left the airport. To think that the whole purpose behind the education of his wife's cousin's son had been the answer to his prayers about Kumari.

Jennifer Harper watched the red-tiled flat roofs and the coconut plantations and the rice paddies dwindle into her past. "Oh yes," she would say casually in Burlington, Vermont. "India. A remarkable country."

Published from COCHIN, MADRAS, MADURAI, BANGALORE, VIJAYAWADA, HYDERABAD, BOMBAY, AHMEDABAD, DELHI, and CHANDIGARH

INDIAN EXPRESS

Largest combined net sales among all daily newspapers in India   Morning F...

Cochin: Saturday September 11 1977

A spooky crematorium

Express News Service

TRIVANDRUM, Sept. 10

An "unclaimed corpse" had to wait more than 72 hours for cremation in the Trivandrum Corporation's new electric crematorium, which was inaugurated yesterday but it had an ominous send-off all right.

The corporation not to be bilked of a chance to demonstrate the crematorium had reportedly kept the unwanted corpse in a city morgue. The corporation's worries that something might go haywire at the last minute say, the corpse melting into thin air or some of the by-standers dropping dead, was not exactly unfounded.

For the plan for constructing an electric crematorium seemed spooked from the start.

The councillor who took the initiative and sponsored the resolution for the crematorium died suddenly. This raised many eyebrows. And the sudden death of the contractor soon after he took up the work struck terror in the minds of the councillors and other contractors. No sooner had another contractor taken up the job, after a good deal of hesitancy and coaxing of course, than a close relation of his died, and suddenly too. And that did it!

There was none to touch "operation electric crematorium" even with a barge pole.

The corporation authorities, though quaking within, nevertheless decided to hold on, unmindful of the host of ghosts which seemed to preempt their every move. They took up the job themselves and with the help of an Indian firm, making use of German technology, built the first electric crematorium in the State, the second in south India and one of the few in the whole of

the country. The ghosts were exorcised, laid to final rest and seemed to have caused no more trouble after that, than put the odd fever in a couple of construction workers.

So, now you can see why the corporation was jittery!

Now, came the worst part of it to "inaugurate" the crematorium in the presence of the Press and thereby make it known to the public. But the Press would not bite the bait, having heard the spooky stories from reliable sources. The cremation, however, had to go on schedule yesterday as the firm's representative was waiting anxiously to push the button, burn the corpse and board the plane.

And it took place without much ado, in the presence of a thin, a very thin, Press. Not to be outdone, the corporation has rescheduled the demonstration for the Press for Tuesday and the Press has started for its worry beads. It remains to be seen where they are going to get another corpse from.

ASHES TO ASHES

CORPSES, THAT IS THE ANSWER. Corpses are my future, thought Krishnankutty with elation and smiled upon his bride Saraswathi as they exchanged the garlands of flowers. She was dazzled by the light of his destiny. It is love, she thought, for she had a college degree in English literature and was an avid reader of Barbara Cartland, Victoria Holt, and other English novelists circulated in paperback among the well-educated and well-born young women of Trivandrum. She recognized the bold and dark passion of the foreign-returned man and quivered with delicious fear.

Krishnankutty took it as an auspicious sign. Corpses, he saw unmistakably, were his *karma* and his fortune. He had experienced a moment of enlightenment and she had perceived it. After the tying of the *tali* they held hands in an ecstasy of mutual misunderstanding. They had seen each other only once before, in the presence of others, and neither had been displeased with the parental choice, but nor had either expected such incandescence. It was the prelude to a night of passion. Krishnankutty had read the *Kama Sutra* while he was a graduate student at M.I.T. – it had been lent to him by his American friend John in a paperback English translation – and that night he laid claim to his Indian heritage. Saraswathi, who had never heard of the *Kama Sutra*, felt that the glorious mysteries of American sex had been revealed to her.

In the morning he told her his plan. It had come to him,

he said, at the instant he had seen her face framed by the bridal garland of jasmine. His American education and his Indian nationalism had merged with the nuptial embrace, and the idea of the electric crematorium had been conceived. It would be the first in the state of Kerala, perhaps the first south of Bombay (though he suspected there was already one in Madras), and certainly one of the few in the whole country.

On the way to the wedding, the groom's party had crossed paths with a funeral procession. The bier was thickly flower-strewn, and even the bearers, carrying it high over their heads, had been weeping. The corpse was that of a beautiful young woman.

Krishnankutty's American friend John – he of the *Kama Sutra* loan – had considered himself fortunate to have his movie camera at the ready, being engaged in recording the procession from the groom's house to that of the bride. In a *frisson* of Eastern excitement, anticipating, he felt, the ultimate perfection of *moksha*, he captured forever on the one reel the continuity of life and death. It was just as Hermann Hesse had intimated in *Siddhartha* – a wedding, a funeral, the beggars at the roadside, the lavish silks and jewels of the bridegroom's party, the river of life flowing on, the vast oneness of it all.

But Krishnankutty's mother, Lakshmi, had been aghast at such an inauspicious encounter. Weeping and trembling, she had begged her husband and son to postpone the wedding lest disaster strike the young couple. Krishnankutty, however, with his American education in electrical engineering, was not worried by such things. Was not this *Chingam*, the auspicious month for marriages? And had not the astrologer consulted by the family indicated that this particular hour on this particular day was the auspicious time?

Clearly then some special thing, good rather than evil, would come of the meeting. And so it had been.

The funeral had reminded Krishnankutty of the final rites for his friend John's mother. She had lain in state, surrounded by flowers, in a room at the funeral home. Krishnankutty had been greatly impressed by the furnishings and wall-to-wall carpet of this room, and by the restrained grief and decorum of the visitors. Later he had marvelled at the quiet simplicity with which, at a certain point in the chapel service at the crematory, the coffin had smoothly rolled out of sight behind a velvet curtain at the unseen touch of a remote control button. The next week he had returned and expressed his professional interest as an engineer, and the management had given him a tour of the crematorium, the discreet workings of which had fascinated him.

Krishnankutty was embarrassed by John's interest in the funeral procession. He strongly suspected that his friend would briefly slip away from the wedding festivities to film the burning of the young girl down on the river bank. He visualized his former acquaintances in Cambridge, Massachusetts watching on screen the blatant leap of flames around the pyre, the muddy river and its filthy excremental banks, the extravagant wailing of the family – all confirming their image of India as a romantically primitive place. It was so unfair. He knew John would not bother to photograph the Shree Kanth, Trivandrum's modern two-storey air-conditioned cinema, which not only showed nightly films in Malayalam, Hindi, and Tamil, but also ran an American movie once a month.

Krishnankutty was, in fact, planning to take his new wife to see the famous James Bond in *Live and Let Die*. He would undertake to open her eyes to the modern world. All these thoughts had been running through his head until the moment she had raised her face to him. He had then experienced a sort of vision in triplicate – the faces of Saraswathi, the recent corpse, and John's mother, all ringed with flowers, hazily intermingling like a multiple-exposure colour slide. It had then come to him that his mission was to establish in Trivandrum an electric crematorium. It was the answer to his newly graduated, newly returned zeal to do something for his country. Not only was it the ideal way to utilize his qualifications, but it would also contribute substantially to the modernization of the city and would incidentally bring him fame and fortune.

John, when confided in a few days later, was appalled by

the plan. He did not have the restless problem-solving mind of an engineer.

"It's practically obscene, Krish," he objected, still full of the beauty of the oneness of all things.

The two friends had met not in university classes, but in the rambling old frame house where they both rented one-bedroom apartments. Since Krishnankutty could not cook, John frequently shared his vegetarian and macrobiotic cuisine. John's family had so much money that it was only natural he should turn from things material to things spiritual. He had been delighted to come to India for his friend's wedding. He decided to stay on. He felt geographically closer to enlightenment, sensed a speeding-up in his search for truth. A crematorium among the coconut groves, it seemed to him, would interfere with the search.

"It's a dreadful idea, Krish," he repeated.

"What do you mean?" asked Krishnankutty, wounded. "You are taking photographs of the lighting of the pyre at the river bank. The water is smelling very bad, and the bank is having much filth, isn't it? Yes, yes. Are these rites suitable for modern educated peoples?"

"Your rites are elemental and beautiful, Krish. One's ashes mingle with the ash and mud of life itself, down there. It is so much purer than the commercial racket of the death industry back home. It would be criminal to change it."

Krishnankutty thought sourly: Those who have already seen their parents croak in style (he was proud of his grasp of American idiom), with the dignity of wall-to-wall carpeting and unseen flame, can afford to be romantic about squalor and the acrid smell of burning flesh.

◇◇◇

Krishnankutty wasted no time. Achuthan Nair, a cousin on his mother's side, was a city councillor. Krishnankutty invited his relative to dinner and revealed to him the splendours of his proposal. He volunteered to draw up designs, in collaboration with an architect, and to submit them to the Corporation of Trivandrum if Achuthan Nair could win that body's support and funding of the scheme.

Achuthan Nair's speech to the Corporation was considered notable, particularly in retrospect. It began with a quotation from Hamlet, which was most impressive. *Alas! poor Yorick*, said Achuthan Nair, inviting the councillors to gaze on the imaginary skull in his hand. How was this sort of noble sentiment possible, he demanded, without lasting mementos of the dead? And even though one's father would return in another form, did not a man cherish the life of his father as he had known it? Would not a small urn of ashes and a plaque bearing the father's name be something of beauty and dignity to be cherished by the family?

There were uneasy tuggings at dhotis and stirrings of sandalled feet, and Divakaran Nambudiripad, an elderly and respected Brahmin, interjected angrily: "Contamination! All is contamination!" The old man rose to his feet. What could be compared, he demanded, with the beauty and dignity of standing on land's end at Cape Comorin where Gandhiji's ashes had been scattered to the elements? What sentiment could the trivial West offer to compare with the religious grandeur of that stormy point where three seas met and where one could be reabsorbed into the universe?

But there were others who were more progressively minded, and they wanted Achuthan Nair to continue. He appealed to Kerala's reputation for enlightened advancement; he alluded to the reformist legacy of His Highness the Maharajah of Travancore; he pointed out that Gandhiji himself had studied in the West and had not been afraid to learn from it; he quoted, with a beautiful cadence, from Keats on the brevity of life, and ended in a crescendo of Milton.

His audience was swept before him. The motion was passed, the money allotted, and a contractor designated. There was a general feeling of well-being, broken only by the mutterings of Divakaran Nambudiripad who warned darkly of the *Kali Yuga*, that Last Age of decline and dissolution.

Two weeks later, when Achuthan Nair died suddenly of a heart attack, Divakaran Nambudiripad felt vindicated and the rest of the Corporation somewhat shaken. But the contractor had been hired and work on the project was already under way. Krishnankutty himself appeared before a special session of the Corporation and spoke with fervour of the rightness, the modernity, and the necessity of the enterprise. With a majority of the city councillors still behind him, he daily supervised the construction site and each nightfall distributed the day's wages to the Harijan labourers.

He invited John to film the work in progress. Not very enthusiastic, John brought his movie camera but was then delighted by the photographic possibilities. He was surprised to see as many women as men engaged in the heavy work. He watched, breathless, running his film, as four men struggled to lift a great piece of rock for the foundations. Painfully they raised it, and then placed it carefully on the head of a squatting woman, very young and beautiful, with only a small coil of braided coconut leaf on her glossy hair to support the rock. When it was properly balanced, the four men let go and the girl very slowly rose to full height and walked across to the foundation, where she again stooped so that several men could lift the rock and place it in position on the wet mortar. This operation was repeated many times and the wall inched its way upward.

"Incredible!" said John. "Beautiful! Tragic!"

"Tragic?" Krishnankutty was startled.

"Such fragile bodies for such brutal work!"

Krishnankutty watched the labourers with surprised interest. Now that he thought about it, it was unusual. He had never seen women on construction sites in America. "Our poor people are very strong," he said proudly. "They are having simple and happy lives."

John was both disturbed and uplifted by the incident. He retreated into contemplation. Suffering in India, he felt, had a sort of ineffable beauty about it, framed as it was by lush rice paddies and coconut groves and the smell of incense and jasmine garlands in the market-place. He took to sitting by the temple baths each day, talking to the old men who sat on the stone steps in the sun. It was a source of grief to him that Kerala (unlike other Indian states) did not permit non-Hindus to enter the temples. Each day he meditated in view of the busily carved *gopuram* of Shree Padmanabhaswamy temple, longing to stand in the presence of Lord Vishnu. He saw less and less of Krishnankutty, found a guru who would help him read the *Vedas*, searched as far afield as Tiruvannamalai to find an ashram that would initiate Westerners as Hindus, after which he decided to set out on foot to Cape Comorin as a pilgrim.

In the third month of Krishnankutty's project, when the exterior walls had risen impressively from the foundations, the building contractor was seriously injured in a fall from the scaffolding, which had been improperly roped together. His back was broken, he lived on for three days of agony, and died murmuring that perhaps Lord Vishnu was offended by the crematorium.

The Corporation was in an uproar. Even Krishnankutty was shaken, yet so certain was he that his inspiration, coming as it had in the high nuptial moment, had been an auspicious one, that he could not easily abandon his dream. He consulted an astrologer, and when that man gave him an unfavourable reading he consulted another one. The second prediction was genial, and armed with this reassurance he again went before the councillors. The task was long and difficult, but he eventually regained the backing of a bare majority.

However, it proved to be impossible to hire a contractor anywhere in the district of Trivandrum. Word had even spread as far north as Quilon, but finally a man from Cochin, who had heard nothing of the matter, agreed to supervise the construction if his accommodation were provided in Trivandrum. Of course he learned the story within days of his arrival, and when word came from Cochin the following week that an aged uncle had died, the man hastily resigned and left the city as quickly as possible.

The more difficult the scheme became, the more determined Krishnankutty grew to see it through to a triumphant conclusion. He spared himself a pointless visit to the nervous elders of the Corporation, but with a single-minded zeal he advertised for a contractor from the adjacent state of Tamil Nadu, hired a man and brought him to Trivandrum at his own expense, gathered a completely different set of Harijan labourers, and saw to it that the contractor ate and slept as a guest at his own house, so that he would have little opportunity to talk to local people. And so the work was finished.

Krishnankutty went to the printer's and ordered fifty neatly scripted white invitation cards. They said: *You are invited to the inauguration of the new electric crematorium of Trivandrum. Conceived and designed by V. Krishnankutty, M.Eng. (Massachusetts Institute of Technology).* He set the date a week in advance to give himself time to find a corpse. He mailed the cards to the councillors of the Corporation of Trivandrum, to representatives of *The Indian Express* and *The Hindu* as well as of the Malayalam newspapers, and to various local dignitaries.

There was some fluster about obtaining a corpse, since recently bereaved families seemed quite unprogressively horrified at the idea. Luckily Saraswathi remembered an old beggar woman who for months had been coming to their door for a daily handful of rice, for weeks had been coughing and spitting blood, and for days had not been seen. Servants were dispatched to make inquiries and they found – alas – the beggar woman's body in a derelict hut. Since there seemed to be no kin to claim her, it was logical that she should have the honour of the first technologically advanced send-off in Trivandrum.

At the appointed hour, Krishnankutty and the beggar woman awaited their guests. Only one person arrived, the reporter from *The Indian Express*. Krishnankutty was incensed, and postponed the ceremonial pushing of the button for a day. He spent the afternoon contacting and visiting as many city councillors as he could. There were many reasons of great import and unavoidable crisis to account for the absences, and of course, they all assured him, they would be present on the morrow. But the next day it was the same, and although it pained Krishnankutty deeply, imperatives of climate and hygiene dictated no further hesitation. History was made before the irreverent eyes of the lone reporter.

❖❖❖

Undaunted, Krishnankutty planned a re-inauguration, more public and inspiring. It was, however, difficult to obtain another corpse. Since the Muslims and Christians did not cremate their dead, one third of the city's population had to be discounted as potential clientele, and even the more progressive Hindu families were wary because of the history of the institution. It then occurred to Krishnankutty that his friend John was Christian, yet John's mother had been cremated. Why was this? Why did Christians in Kerala bury their dead, while for Christians in America the manner of disposal was apparently optional? Perhaps the answer to this problem lay in a re-education of the Christian community in Trivandrum. Once the public became used to the idea of the crematorium, once there had been a significant number of uneventful funerals, Krishnankutty was convinced that his difficulties would be over.

❖❖❖

He went to visit the heads of the three leading churches of the Christian community of Trivandrum – the Syrian Orthodox, the Roman Catholic, and the Church of South India. The Syrian priest, who did not of course believe in the caste system, but nevertheless considered the Syrian Christians to be superior to the Nair caste (of which Krishnankutty was a member), received him frostily. Since it was well known to the Nairs that in Kerala their caste was of a greater and nobler antiquity than even that of the Brahmin immigrants from the Aryan north, Krishnankutty was not impressed. The priest explained matters to him as to a child. American Christians, he said, were living in a state of serious theological error. The Syrians, a people of great antiquity and nobility – he stressed this meaningfully – were the preservers of original historical truth, and would never deviate from ancient custom. Since the time of their founder St. Thomas the Apostle, whose hallowed bones rested in Madras, they had buried their dead.

Samuel Varghese, the Roman Catholic priest, was a man of Indo-Portuguese descent from Goa. He was more courteous, deferring politely to Krishnankutty. He explained that since Our Lord himself had been buried, and since Christians awaited the final resurrection of the body, Catholic Christians all over the world, including America, considered burial the only acceptable final rite in the sight of God.

There were two equally important congregations of the Church of South India in Trivandrum. Theoretically they had merged thirty years previously in the union of all Protestant denominations, but in practice they had little to do with each other. The English-speaking high-born congregation was the legacy of the Anglican missionaries of the British Raj, and still used the Episcopalian liturgy. The bishop told Krishnankutty that cremation could never be contemplated because there was no provision for it in the Book of Common Prayer.

The pastor of the poorer Malayalam-speaking congregation, the Reverend Jesudas, had been trained by the evangelical Congregationalists of the London Missionary Society. He conceded that while there was no express theological injunction against cremation, within India it did of course have the connotation of a Hindu ritual. And Christians, he said, were a people called to be different, to bear witness to the gospel of Christ. He quoted from the King James version of the Bible. "Come ye out from among them, saith the Lord, and be ye separate and touch not the unclean thing." For Christians, he said as gently as possible, Hindu rituals were – metaphorically speaking, of course – unclean.

❖❖❖

All this was very confusing, and not very promising, for Krishnankutty. But he felt that hope was not completely excluded with respect to the former London Missionary Society people. Perhaps if John, who was of that same Protestant tradition, were to talk with the pastor, something might be achieved. So he went to find his friend John, whom he had not seen during the many months of his construction project. But John, it seemed, had bent as new rice before the monsoon of enlightenment, and it was several days before he was found in a small and wretched hut alongside the temple. He was barely recognizable.

"Are you ill?" Krishnankutty asked in alarm.

"I am part of the cosmos," answered John. "I am not my body, which does not concern me."

There was an unwholesome yellowish tinge to John's skin and a dreadful odour about his body. Krishnankutty became aware of a puddle of bloodied excrement trickling from the straw mat on which John sat. Hepatitis, he thought with alarm.

"John, my dear friend, you are very ill. I am calling a taxi and taking you immediately to the Medical College Hospital."

John gazed from his doorway, across the expanse of sacred water, to the towering *gopuram* of the temple.

"In the presence of Lord Vishnu, I am safe," he replied. "I don't wish to go to a hospital."

"This is being very foolish, John. Perhaps you are not trusting our hospitals? I assure you that Medical College Hospital is not inferior to excellent hospitals in America. We are going now, isn't it?"

"No! I will remain in the presence of the Lord."

"John, John! I am a Vishnavite. Each day I make *puja* to Lord Vishnu. Yet I would not do this! No modern and educated Vishnavite would do this. You cannot do this. You are coming with me."

"I have taken a vow to meditate at this shrine of Lord Vishnu for thirty days. I cannot leave. Would you have me break a vow?"

Nothing could be done about a vow. Krishnankutty went home

in considerable consternation. Each day he visited his friend, bringing rice and fruit which John was unable to swallow. He then brought bowls of *payasam*, a thin sweet gruel, but still John vomited as soon as he had eaten. He was now feverish and often unconscious, but adamantly rejected all pressure to enter a hospital. Who can release himself from a solemn vow made to the Lord of the Universe?

He is dying, thought Krishnankutty. He is *dying*!

At first unbidden and pushed aside with shame, the thought came to him that John would be his next corpse. But after all, why not? Certainly he knew that John had no objections to cremation. He did not of course want his friend to die, but if fate decreed....

"I have a last request, Krish," said John weakly from his straw mat. Krishnankutty bent solicitously over his friend.

"You are not to contact my relatives or send my body back to America. Mankind is my family, the universe is my home. My ashes must mingle with Truth, here in India."

"Yes, yes. I promise," said Krishnankutty sadly. He could see the invitation cards, discreetly edged in black.

"I want to be carried from the temple to the river bank, and it is my wish that you, my dear friend, you alone, should light my funeral pyre."

"Ahh, John, John! I beg you, do not ask this of me. Consider the cause of progress...."

"It is my final wish that you scatter my ashes at Cape Comorin and let the three oceans carry them to the ends of the earth."

Sadly Krishnankutty kept vigil while the universe, by subtle rearrangement, absorbed John. Then he crossed the street to the temple flower sellers.

It is my *karma*, he sighed.

He placed a garland on the corpse.

THE DARK WOOD

A NGELA turned off the car radio, not wanting to hear about Princess Margaret and boyfriend. Not at high speed on the turnpike with one death behind her and another one waiting ahead.

She wondered: why do I always pick the wrong men? She was surely second only to Her Highness in that respect, although she had been sufficiently adroit never to marry her mistakes and had been spared the embarrassment of having her terminal romances splashed across the international press.

And of course her work helped. She could become so absorbed in cases that she would not remember if there was anyone waiting for her at home or not. When she thought "home" she meant whichever one-and-a-half-room studio her Bokharas, pillows, and plants were gracing at that moment. She travelled light. Decorating style: expensive stark. Portable elegance. Nothing that could not be relocated in three trips of her MG with car rack. She moved in and out of her life.

On the turnpike she played with her blinkers like a magician, changing lanes, moving, weaving, dodging. Disengaging. Brendan, however, kept circling her consciousness like the foggy rings around Saturn. Brendan and his children, Brendan and his crisis, Brendan and his importunate pleading eyes – as persistent as that green Chrysler dogging her, arrogantly suffusing her rear-view mirror. With deft timing she slithered into a momentary space in the next lane then back into the fast lane two cars ahead. The Chrysler, she saw with pleasure, was a dwindling green dot in her mirror.

She thought with contempt: all my men have been tail-gaters. Clinging. Hampering.

Well, there it was. Death of another relationship. She could not be encumbered with the debris of Brendan's life when her work was so important, people depending on her, matters of life and death. There had been, of course, grey spaces of betrayal in his eyes. That was the way it was with her men. Impossible demands and messy endings.

But this was misting away at the periphery of her mind. She changed lanes, jockeying for the exit. She always stayed in the fast lane until the last possible minute, defying entanglements, winning the off ramp. She parked in her reserved space at the hospital.

❖❖❖

Odours come coded. The brackish tang of seaweed can sting the nostrils and suddenly one is feeling for a pitted anklet of scars and hearing an old scream hurtle off the rocks, childhood blood spurting from oyster shells.

Angela smelled the familiar wave of disinfectant, bed pans, assorted medicinal fumes, and felt invigorated. Other people might turn faint at that smell but Angela inhaled power. Within its ambience she had a certain licence to bind and loose. She made mortal arrangements.

Her case-load was heavy but it was the latest admission which most immediately concerned her. The bed of Beatrice Grossetti floated in its own haze of mustiness. The smell of the last century, thought Angela; of oiled furniture and old photographs; the smell of a person long unused.

Only a small fetal arc disturbed the bedding but the face on the pillow was gnome-like and ancient. Angela glanced at her clipboard. This was the clinical data: Beatrice Grossetti was seventy years old. No living relatives. Weight: eighty pounds.

The ancient eyes of the child-body opened.

Angela said briskly, "Good morning, Miss Grossetti."

"*Mrs.* Grossetti. Are you the doctor?"

"Not a medical doctor. I'm here to help you sort out anything that might be worrying you."

The eyes closed again. "I thought the clergy did that."

"They do, if that's what you prefer. Would you like to see a priest?"

"No." Mrs. Grossetti's eyes, startled and skittish as dragonflies, darted out from cover. "I don't know ... perhaps later.... Is it so urgent?"

She was wounded now, a cornered animal.

Angela, releaser of traps, liberator of caged spirits, sat beside the bed.

"No rush," she said.

She was confident that the timing depended on her patient and herself. None of her cases had ever gone before they were ready. She had a certain knack, and the dying have instincts of their own.

"You will know when. And I will be with you."

Mrs. Grossetti's face contorted itself into what would have been a scream if any sound had come out. She clutched at Angela who took both gnarled hands between her own, leaning forward to press them against her cheek.

"It's all right, it's all right," she murmured. "You're not alone. I am with you."

"How can *knowing* ... how can just the *knowing*...?" The voice of Mrs. Grossetti struggled to assert itself over some rushing undertow. "Two days ago everything was ... *usual*. Slow and weak ... just the usual slow and weak ... just age. I watered my geraniums and my tomatoes. They're ripening so I have to watch out for the pigeons.... I grow them in my window box you know, they'll be ready in about ten days.... And then my ... Mr. Bernstein, the man in my little supermarket ... he said – such a nice gentleman – he said: 'I'm worried about you, Beatrice. You're looking a little thinner every time I see you. I wish you'd see a doctor.' And just to please him, you know...."

There was a long pause while Mrs. Grossetti's forces deployed themselves. They tapped some wild energy of insight and she sat up abruptly.

"But nothing has changed! Just *knowing* cannot make any difference. Nothing has changed. I want my tomatoes."

She slumped back wearily.

"Couldn't I go home to my tomatoes?" she pleaded. "Don't you think I could just stay home until...." She turned to the wall. "If anything is going to happen, I'd rather be home. I *would* like to see my tomatoes ripen. I'm frightened here. Couldn't I go home? Nothing has happened, except the knowing. Couldn't I go home, please? Just *knowing* can't make any difference."

"It always does make a difference. For everyone."

"I want to *un*-know! I only came as a favour to Mr. Bernstein. Now I want to go away again. Couldn't I, please? Please...?"

After a while Angela gently freed herself from the fingers closed tightly on sleep and hope.

It was well known to the friends of Dr. Angela Carson that she did not like to be paged for personal calls while she was at the hospital. Although she did not explain it in so many words, it seemed to her as obscene as surreptitiously reading a paperback (neatly hidden inside the prayer book) at a funeral service. Consequently when she was summoned to the phone she knew it would be Brendan. No one else, at the moment anyway, would be so rash and desperate. Jacob would have done the same thing once. And then Charles. But there it was again. Birds of a feather.

"Angela, we have to talk. I can't believe you meant what you said yesterday. I'll pick you up at the hospital this evening and we'll go out for dinner. You've been over-reacting because you're overworked."

"Brendan, you know I hate to be called here. Anything you might have to say is irrelevant to me while I am working."

He said wearily: "Angela, I fail to see how some sort of semi-human robot can help the dying."

"Goodbye, Brendan."

"Angela! For god's sake! I don't even understand what happened. What are you afraid of?"

"I'm not afraid of anything. I have responsibilities."

"But a visit, for heaven's sake! Do you want me to surrender the right ever to see my children?"

"Of course not. But you can't expect me to get involved in that sort of draining familial situation."

"What's draining about a visit that's already *over*? You're being so irrational. . . ."

She replaced the receiver delicately on its hook.

In all honesty, she thought, I cannot blame myself for this fiasco. She had not, after all, been anticipating overnight visits from his children. Infrequent or otherwise.

Angela's profession placed her under a heavy moral obligation. The dying cannot postpone the gathering up of loose ends and the settling of accounts. She owed it to her cases to lead an uncluttered life, to be capable of undivided attention, compassion, total commitment.

◇◇◇

When Angela reached the door of Beatrice Grossetti's room, a young intern was moving a stethoscope about her body, pausing and listening, his face creased with solemn inner deliberation. As though he were sounding an old hull for seaworthiness, Angela thought.

"Doctor?" asked Mrs. Grossetti in a small apologetic voice. "What can you tell me?"

As she spoke she reached out tentatively, supplicatingly, and touched his arm. The young intern flinched, moving aside to put his equipment back in its case.

"You're in good hands, Mrs. Grossetti." He smiled paternally. "We'll take expert care of you here."

He nodded at Angela as he left the room, flushing slightly

before the direct baleful impact of her eyes. It was curious, she thought with anger, the way so many people cringed from contact with death. As though it were catching. As though the patient were already a leper, an outcast, no longer one of us. She had seen it in doctors, relatives, visitors.

The familiar look of shame suffused Mrs. Grossetti's face, the embarrassment of imposing on the living. Angela saw the tears and instinctively leaned over and kissed her gently on the forehead.

"Tell me about yourself, Mrs. Grossetti. Tell me how you came to have your beautiful name. Beatrice has always been one of my favourites, especially if you pronounce it the Italian way."

"I can't blame them, I suppose. It's natural, isn't it?" replied Mrs. Grossetti who walked down her own paths. "You are different though. I suppose you see so many ... so much of this ... it seems ordinary to you."

"I do see a lot. Perhaps the difference is the doctors are fighting *against* death. But you see I share it, I stay with my patients. No one is left alone."

"Are you afraid of being alone?"

Angela was disconcerted. "No! Oh no. Not me. I don't want *you* to feel alone."

"I would feel less alone with my geraniums and tomatoes than here. It is very cruel to keep me here. I've lived, you know. I've seen a lot. Buried my only son (he was just a child) and my husband. And a good many friends. I've seen a lot of ... not as many as you perhaps, but I'm no stranger to ... at least, I didn't think I was."

Mrs. Grossetti drifted in and and out of sleep. Angela had other cases to attend to and she came and went. But she checked with Beatrice every hour. She had an instinct about these things.

Sometimes the frail body stirred and whimpered, and Angela would sit and hold her hand.

"Mrs. Grossetti? I'm here. Is there anything you want?"

"Beatrice. My name is Beatrice."

"It's such a beautiful name."

"My father loved Dante. He taught in a college. My father, that is. You know Dante's Beatrice?"

"Yes indeed. I took one whole course on him in college myself. The professor used to make us recite the Italian aloud because it sounded so beautiful. *I' son Beatrice che ti faccio andare....*"

"Is that the part where she meets him in paradise?"

"No. It's at the beginning, in the dark wood. When he was lost and afraid."

"Such a luxury. To believe there was somebody waiting for him.... And then finally all that light and peace. Do you believe it?"

Angela said soothingly, as to a child: "Perhaps, perhaps. I don't know."

"I used to. I wish I still could."

"That's not so important. I do know that death itself is a moment of joy and peacefulness. I can *promise* you. I have *seen* it over and over again."

"But after that you can't know, can you, doctor? I wish I'd never been a Catholic. It keeps you scared up to your very last breath."

"Do you want to see a priest?"

"Not yet, not yet. I want to see my tomatoes ripen."

Beatrice slept again and Angela went about her rounds.

The surfacing into speech was less frequent, the exchanges with Beatrice more fragmented as the afternoon wore on.

"It is so strange," she said once, quite suddenly, "to think of the tomatoes ripening next week without me. Ripening and rotting all by themselves."

Acceptance, Angela thought. The final stage. "Shall I bring a priest now?"

Beatrice opened her eyes and turned to face Angela.

"You're in such a hurry, doctor. Determined to see me off properly, aren't you?"

"You are a Catholic, Beatrice. It is customary...."

"Yes, yes. For the final promises. And will you believe him? Will you find the promises reassuring?"

Angela, caught off guard, almost said: I'm not the one who is dying.

Instead she said: "It is what *you* believe that matters, Beatrice."

"It doesn't matter to you yet, doctor. Things *are*, things *are* – whatever we believe. I believed I was healthy two days ago."

She sighed and seemed to lapse back into sleep. Angela was about to go but Beatrice seized her hand.

"Don't go, doctor. I'm afraid. I'm so frightened."

Angela slipped her arm under the trembling shoulders. On impulse she raised Beatrice and cuddled her as though she were a small child. The figure felt light as an infant. Angela rocked back and forth on the bed, crooning softly.

As Beatrice slithered back across the hazy border into unconsciousness, her fingers curled themselves around Angela's wrist. The head, under its wispy halo of silver grey, sank a little more heavily against Angela's shoulder. Angela made no attempt to extricate herself. She continued to rock back and forth, singing a lullaby.

◇◇◇

The eyes of the night-shift nurse widened. She stood indecisively in the doorway with her tray of medications. Dr. Angela Carson seemed oblivious to her presence so she left again. It was something, she thought with wonder, to recount at coffee break.

An orderly arrived with a note. Angela surfaced as from a great depth, swaying slightly, to read it.

"Tell Brendan ... tell the gentleman I can't come down," she said. "I have to work all night."

She went on stroking Beatrice's hair, rocking, singing.

◇◇◇

Shortly after midnight, Beatrice began to struggle.

"No!" she cried out. "No! No! No!"

"Shall I bring a priest?"

"No! No!"

Angela held her. "It's all right, Beatrice. I'm here. It's all right."

Beatrice was gasping, scooping in air with a greedy bronchial rattling. Her body tightened and bucked. Angela buzzed for the nurse and for emergency help, whispering caressingly: "Let go, Beatrice. Just relax and let go now. It's easy, it's peaceful, it's not worth hanging on. You're *there* now."

Convulsion.

With wholly unexpected energy, Beatrice slapped Angela across the face.

"You are making me sick." Her words flew like grapeshot, low and deadly. "If it's so easy, why don't you try it?" And then, like a baleful Cassandra: "Look! I see the bones behind your face. Go away, you fool, go away, go away, go away!"

Angela drew back from the crescendo of hysteria. She felt disoriented, drunken as a ship snagged suddenly on an uncharted rock. She had a sensation of internal puncture, of ominous seepage. She made way for nurses and the doctor, she moved like a sleep-walker down the corridor.

The cry of Beatrice, a rattling network of panic and malevolent laughter, billowed after her like a vast cobweb, endlessly sticky, grotesquely caressing, wisping away gradually before the blessings of sedation.

◇◇◇

Angela sat trembling behind the wheel of her car, poised at the mouth of the entry ramp, unable to propel herself into the slipstream of the turnpike. Already she was reproaching herself for a moment of professional inadequacy. Never before had she allowed one of her cases to die alone. This, she saw clearly, was the cause of her distress.

So late at night the traffic was thin but it hurtled by at a menacing speed, headlamps glaring in the dark like burning eye sockets. There seemed to be a fog of hazard, randomness, in the night air. Suddenly she was astonished that she had miraculously survived so many circuits of that urban racetrack.

Another car purred up the entry ramp behind her and its lights bathed her in gold. She was swamped by a panic compelling as nausea. From out of the heart of the radiance came a rhythm of horns, stern as the trumpets of angels. Beatrice stood on her dark side, mocking.

Angela felt herself to be ten years old again, teetering at the tip of the highest diving board, not knowing how to dive, distant figures far below calling encouragement, the line of people on the ladder rungs growing impatient, the board swaying precariously, no return possible.

She put her car suddenly into reverse, swerved crazily around the vehicle behind her, backed off the ramp, and returned to the parking lot at the hospital where she collapsed over her steering wheel, shaking violently.

The chill air of the parking lot sobered her. But even before she located the night nurse she knew she would be too late.

"It was very peaceful," the nurse said. "She never regained consciousness."

Of course, Angela thought, it could be explained by malevolence. Revenge against youth, against the living. Statistically it was not significant. All the others, every single one, had gone gently, slipping quietly into beatitude, grateful for her presence.

There was, she knew from years of experience, a certain amount of choice at the end. As regards timing. Beatrice had chosen to deny her the last peaceful coda. Just this once she had missed out on the epiphany. Yes.

As she grew calmer she went back to her car, but when she tried to start it the violent trembling returned. She hugged herself, shivering, and waited for the malaise to pass.

SOME HAVE CALLED THEE
MIGHTY AND DREADFUL

WHAT FASCINATED ME MOST when I woke on the Sunday morning was the deviousness, the sheer cunning of the lower levels of my mind. I had felt the steering wheel under my hands, tightened my fingers around it, *shaken* it. So much material evidence, tangible, proof that I was not dreaming. And that in itself astonished me – that within the dream I should have suspected I was dreaming and applied tests.

Having verified that it was not, indisputably *not* a dream, I drove on down the bumpy country road in the crazy yellow car, passing weathered barns, swerving for a bovine jay-walker or two, gulping the honeysuckle air, exultant. I was exceptional, chosen, blessed. I was possibly the only living being to know what I knew.

Then I drove into Sunday morning and the smell of slept-in sheets. Glanced urgently backward across the waking. Held the fading euphoric eyes of the car driver watching me through the windshield with the intensity of the Ancient Mariner, sadder, wiser, fading.

❖❖❖

"Remember Quincy?" asked Joey.

"What's Quincy?"

"Our kitten that got run over."

"I don't remember a kitten. Was I borned then?"

"Yes, but you were too little. I meant Mommy. Remember Quincy, Mommy?"

I said cautiously: "He went to your Grandfather's castle."

Joey flushed angrily. "That was kid stuff. A car ran over Quincy in the parking lot. All his guts squished out. Daddy and I buried him. There was blood all over. You would have throwed up, Caroline, but you were too little to understand."

"I bet you cried. I bet you were a big cry-baby," chanted Caroline, humiliated not to have participated in the frightful mystery of Quincy's spilled guts.

"So what? He was just a baby kitten. And who cried last night, eh? Who threw up last night?"

Joey left the room abruptly. Caroline clung to my arm as though it might disappear and began to weep again.

So Joey's Grandfather was already jettisoned, withering before the cynical scrutiny of the second grade. Omnipotent and benevolent, he had once loomed far larger than the shadowy absent grandfather who lived across the ocean. This one, always accessible to Joey, lived in a castle, host to a fluid and fabulous assortment of guests, possessor of all desired objects – real jewelled swords, a canoe, a rocket ship, and a Saint Bernard, among other things. On the day after Quincy's death, Joey had asked for permission to disinter the kitten. It was necessary to take it to the castle, where his Grandfather had a set of magic band-aids that healed all wounds. Desolate for two days after the refusal of his request, contemptuous and furious toward well-meaning explanations, he came down to breakfast on the third morning in a cloud of beatitude. He had visited his Grandfather, and whom did we suppose he had seen skittering playfully across the castle courtyard?

✧✧✧

On Monday the children wanted reassurances. Even Joey, who affected to be a little embarrassed by them these days, clung to the goodbye hug. Caroline asked: "Will you be here when we come home from school?"

"Of course."

"I'm taking my special ruby-coloured glass to school. That piece I found in the garden. I'm going to give it to Lissa."

"I don't expect Melissa will be at school today," I told them.

◇◇◇

Only Saturday, after the circus, we had trailed along the border of the city park, Cassandra and I in front, the children in a sticky bliss of cotton candy, giggles, and communal reminiscence strung out behind us.

"Remember the clown trying to start up the old car?" Joey was calling back over his shoulder to Caroline and Laura. They were walking arm in arm. I remember that, grateful. They might have been quarrelling as they often do. Did. Arm in arm, Laura's cheek pink and wet where Caroline's cotton candy grazed it.

We stopped in the park to let the children play. Cassandra's voice came lazily from deep in the grass. "Winter seems an impossibility now."

"Like a bad dream," I said, still tasting its aftermath, but breathing in the smell of crushed clover.

"I won't go into a decline like that next winter," she said. "I mean really. I've climbed up to *somewhere* and I won't fall back again. Freedom. It's like the clover. In February you can't believe it will ever come. But it does. It's real."

She grasped a handful of tall grass and clover, caressing it as one might the phallus of a husband or lover. "Look at Laura," she said. Our eyes zigzagged with the unsynchronized swinging of Laura and Caroline. "She'll be in school next year. There'll never be another winter like this last one. I won't need to dream of a lover. I'll have *myself* again, and a job, next winter."

I smiled sourly, jealous of her confidence. I'd had myself *ad nauseam* that winter, but neither job nor lover had dropped into my questing life. Still, summer had come for us all indiscriminately, winners and losers.

"I suppose we'll look back on our journals some day and laugh. Or cringe."

"Oh, the journals," she said disdainfully. We were both embarrassed to have been embroiled in such a predictable crisis, such a stock-in-trade of the women's magazines, the death-wish apathy of the snowed-in mother-knotted months.

"I can positively say right now that I intend to cram a lot into the rest of my life."

"Me too," I said lamely, willing myself to believe it.

"In fact," she expatiated to the clover and the summer, "I would be furious, absolutely furious, if I died now."

Big deal, I thought. All this energy of rage and ambition. If I could tap just a fraction of it.

◇◇◇

Later, in the middle of the welter of bubble bath and sticky bodies, the phone rang.

"Can you get that?" I called downstairs and went on lathering Caroline's hair. Joey complained that she was taking up too much room, splashed water at her. Caroline screamed that she had soap in her eyes.

"Remember the clown in the old car?" I said.

It worked. Laughter.

"This is the way he walked," chuckled Joey, bouncing from buttock to buttock, slithering in the soapy tub. Then Caroline was spluttering: "Daddy! Daddy! There was this clown – let *me* tell, Joey – this clown with an old car – Mommy, make Joey be quiet. *I'm* telling daddy...."

"Want to take over?" I glanced back at the doorway where he stood, ashen. "What's wrong?"

Cacophony of splashing, competitive shrieking, high-pitched laughter.

"Shut up!" he bellowed.

It was like an obscenity, so unexpected. His words plummeted into the sudden hush.

"There's been an accident. A car. Driver drunk or something. Cassandra. Laura's in hospital, critically injured. Melissa's okay. I'd better go to John. He was calling from the hospital."

"Cassandra? What about Cassandra?"

"Killed."

A space. Nothing. Something lurching.

Then a quick flurry to get Caroline to throw up into the toilet, not the bathtub.

◇◇◇

On the late news I saw witnesses interviewed. Fifteen minutes, I figured. Fifteen minutes after we left the playground it had happened. We had walked south, away from the park. They had walked east along the park boundary for several blocks.

"Oh my god, it was horrible. Horrible!" a woman was saying. "Suddenly this car gunned out of nowhere. From somewhere behind me. . . . I don't know. One second I saw the woman and the little girls – then I could only see one little girl. . . . And the car wrapped around a tree."

A grotesque death, the announcer explained. Cassandra's body had been dragged fifty yards to be mashed between car and tree. Melissa, evidently, had received only a glancing blow. Laura's body had ricocheted off the car and crumpled into the grass.

◇◇◇

The children had wanted to sleep in the same room, had required crooning and lullabies till they fell asleep. Caroline's body shuddered in the grip of dreams. The glaring eye of the night-light watched, unwinking.

There had been another phone call from the hospital where they were waiting out the hours of Laura's surgery. There were ruptured organs. She would probably die.

I sat in the rocker in the children's room, afraid to leave them. It seemed very cold, I kept shivering. I thought about the clover that might still be visibly crushed from Cassandra's hands. I thought about the fifty yards. Then I remembered something else. That party, a month ago, where someone had been discussing Kübler-Ross – the cases of people who had been clinically dead for a number of minutes, who later knew how many electrocardiac shocks their "dead" bodies had received, who recalled being outside their bodies, watching, having a sense of urgency about getting back.

It was exciting grist for discussion, more enthralling than chess, until suddenly Cassandra spoke with the intensity of someone who has managed to rip off a gag in the last second before suffocation. Staccato rushes of sound.

"What is the *point* of this conversation? Is it to make us all terrified of death? To make us sweat for the rest of our lives, wondering what will happen *after*? What we will *know*?"

There were murmurs, coughing, disavowals. That fluid instinct that fills up social abysses, blurs their edges. Moments later, drained and trembling slightly, Cassandra was blushing, apologetic, embarrassed by her outburst.

❖❖❖

I would be furious, absolutely furious, if I died now. Those fifty yards. Were they intense with knowledge, recognizing death, seeing the distorted bundle of Laura, reaching for the bereft Melissa? Knowing, knowing, raging. Yes, that is what I fear, that is what claws at my gut, crams my throat with vomit. She died angry. She is still angry.

I shiver. I think of Laura's bedside. She is there, angry, impotent, anguished. This is irrational. I am gagging on something, the acrid taste of guilt, responsibility. No, this is not coherent, not a time for clear perspectives. But if we had lain in the clover another five minutes. Or five minutes less. If I had invited them back to our house. If I had only tilted time a few minutes to one side or the other. This is shock. Of course I am not responsible. Life is random, brutally indifferent. The clover. Fifteen minutes. Fifty yards.

How can I not be responsible?

❖❖❖

I was lying in a large hospital ward. It was segregated, no visitors allowed. Only the terminally ill came there. They permitted us our last little pleasures, our self-indulgences.

We could go downstairs, below ground level, to the library. It was a mezzanine floor, with thick opaque glass catwalks threading between the stacks. Just like the library I worked in once. I spent most of my time down there, it was so peaceful, every conceivable book available.

Readers milled around, brushed one another silently, smiled, all rather indistinguishable in loose white hospital gowns. The other ones, the grey ones, never took their own books from the shelves. Someone placed them open and waiting on their carrels.

The grey ones moved lightly and gracefully. When they looked up, someone, one of us, would turn the page.

"Why do you never fetch your own books, or turn your own pages?" I asked one.

"We are from downstairs," the grey one answered.

"Downstairs?"

"After you leave the ward you go downstairs, below the library."

"After you leave the ward?" I repeated it slowly. I reached out to touch.

There was nothing. Just so, I recalled, had Dante tried to clasp Virgil. "What is it like, downstairs?"

"It is ... a little cold, but very peaceful. You will like it. We can come up here to the library any time we want. Only we have to depend on one of you to take down the books."

"Do you know many people down there?"

"Of course."

"Do you know...? Is there someone named Cassandra?"

"Ah yes, Cassandra. She just arrived. She will be sleeping, it will be a few days before she can come up here and talk to you. But you can visit her now."

The grey one led me down a narrow iron staircase. Downstairs it was chilly, like a wine cellar. There were neat rows of stacks, with large file drawers instead of books. The grey one pulled out a drawer and I saw Cassandra, in repose, not at all damaged, an ice princess of a beauty to make princes rash with thorn thickets.

At a party once someone had said to me: "You two are unnerving, you know. I mean, one expects philosophers' wives to be dowdy, somehow. But look at you! And Cassandra! My god!"

"I'll tell you that one later, in the library," I said to the sleeping Cassandra.

But I never saw her in the library. The impossible happened, I got better. It was a problem, no one had ever been released from the ward before, except to go downstairs. They made me promise not to tell.

I drove away in a little yellow sports car, delirious with life. Nothing to be scared about ever. Books, peace, no pain, no terror. God, what luck, to be perhaps the only human being who actually knew.... But if it should be only a dream? It wasn't a dream. I could smell lilacs and honeysuckle, I could feel the wheel, solid and smooth, under my hands. The leather upholstery had an embossed textured grain, tactile.

"Melissa *was* at school," Caroline told me.

Joey was running a fever at bedtime.

"Do you think Cassandra was maybe wicked?" he asked me privately.

"Whatever do you mean?"

"I mean, do you think maybe she was a robber? Or maybe killed someone? Or maybe did dreadful things no one knew about, only Melissa?"

"Joey! Of course not! Cassandra was killed by a crazy car driver. Did you think she was being punished for something?"

"No." Blankly. "But Melissa doesn't love her. I think she must have hated her. I think she's glad she's dead."

"Did Melissa tell you that?"

"No."

"What makes you think such a thing?"

He burst into tears, burrowing into my arms.

"She was *playing* at recess. She was *laughing*. Like nothing happened."

The words became tangled and lost in body-shaking sobs.

On Monday night, John told us about her will. All the specifics.

She had set them down legally, years ago. No embalming, no open casket, a plain pine coffin. Does everyone do that, make arrangements? At our age? It had never occurred to me. No viewing – my god, in the circumstances. . . .

There were too many imponderables. *I would be furious.* . . . Fifteen minutes. Perhaps after any death it happens, retrospective significance. If I died tomorrow, would they say: she read Plath and Sexton – strange! But the outburst at the party? The will? Did she know? Did she make it happen? What is a coincidence?

On Tuesday the funeral was some sort of catharsis, of exhaustion if nothing else.

"Mommy, why are you shaking?" Caroline asked me at the cemetery.

I held a hand of each child, their faces were red and swollen, they shivered. But they had chosen to come, yes, they belonged, had a right.

"I'm not. I'm just sad. I'm missing her. I'm worrying about Laura and Melissa and John," I whispered, trembling, smelling clover, tasting earth.

"Does she *feel* that? Does she know they're shovelling dirt?" Joey asked.

"No. It's like when you're asleep. Nothing. It's just like being nothing."

"I have nightmares," he said uncertainly.

Ah, but in that sleep of death, what dreams may come!

"Not when you're dead. No dreams. Never. Nothing."

They were reassured.

I have watched people since, carefully, with calculating assessing eye. The old people next door, they must feel it coming. Never a sign, never a tremor.

"Another friend of mine passed away last week," the old lady tells me. I watch like a hawk. "We were at school together." She sighs and smiles. "Ah well, we're all getting on." She says it like a benediction.

Perhaps it has unhinged me. Am I a coward, simply that? I admit nothing. No one admits anything. Perhaps after all everyone has a closet theology, a resurrection trump. Let them have their Grandfather's castles, whatever helps.

Nothing helps me. I feel the weight of damp black clay pressing on her, on me. These are my night thoughts, shameful. If I could only stop feeling Cassandra's rage. Beside Laura, white, fragile, tented, machine-monitored, I think: she is raging with grief. By Melissa, lost and pensive, I think: she is straining against the bonds of her absence, furious.

If I could only be certain it was nothingness. No knowledge. No dreams. I walk around with the taste of earth sour on my tongue, growing my cancer of fear, my terminal illness.

AFTER THE FALL

THE DAY THE AMARYLLIS FELL her husband was at a conference in another city. She was glad to be alone. Lately she had even been keeping the children out of the studio, having become uneasy and selfconscious in the plant's extravagant presence.

She clamped a large sheet of paper to the easel and did a quick preliminary sketch in charcoal. Tentative title: *Hubris in the Vegetable Kingdom*. It was the inexorability of self-destruction she was after, the heavy suddenness of those three trumpet flowers tumbling down under their own weight like a blasted carillon of bells. Ask not for whom the amaryllis tolls.

She changed the paper and sketched a single detail in overblown scale, magnifying the bruised bending point of the stalk. Probing the wound for clues.

The stricken flowers trailing across her work-table suddenly jangled like doomsday bells. She grabbed another sheet, clipped it up, drew the sound. Chiaroscuro of discord. The shrieking would not be laid to rest. She took a new sheet, drew it again feverishly, concentrating this time on the tormented mouth of a single flower.

Silence.

Relieved, she laid out the four drawings side by side on her work-table. Not too bad, but so much had been missed. The buckled stalk bleeding green opalescent sap. The murky bruise staining the red-streaked petals. She needed colour.

Scooping up the finished sheets, she dropped them into the back of the amaryllis portfolio, a bulging record of three months' worth of changes – changes not even suspected by heedless people who threw out their Christmas plants when the first blooms withered.

The fallen flowers screamed again, strident with self-pity – an interminable wail like an alarm bell or a tintinnabulation of raw nerve ends. She snatched up a fresh sheet, dropped it, picked it up, clamped it, tore open her pastels. The sound was horribly trapped inside her head, insistent as a panicked mosquito caught in the ear. She drew the violent flowers but the ringing went on unabated. One might go mad from it.

Was it the telephone, she wondered?

She reached for it, hooking it under her chin, changing sheets.

"I've been calling all morning," he said. "I thought you must be out."

Him. His voice. And for months she had waited. Sweat trickled across her upper lip and she brushed it with the back of her hand, smearing her face with charcoal and pastel dust.

"What are you doing?" As though he still had a right to know.

"I'm drawing the amaryllis. The one you gave me for Christmas. It keeps changing."

Even now a translucent bruise, a wan greenness the colour of undersea moss, was seeping along the stalk in both directions from the breaking point. Pastels were inadequate. She reached for her watercolours.

"My husband is out of town for a few days," she said. Casually.

There was a silence. She watched the pale stalk bleeding greenly.

"Actually," she said, "this is not a convenient time to talk. The gallery has commissioned five lithographs. I'm absorbed in the preliminary sketches. Other things seem, you know, extraneous."

She hung up. She was absorbed, in fact, in the essence of change. A momentous project. In the last few minutes the bruised underside of a petal had mutated infinitesimally toward colourlessness. She could only hope to capture it with water-colour washes, eventually with the lithograph washes.

He might or might not come over of course. At least he knew she was alone if he wanted to make anything of it. Why had he called anyway, after all this time? Not that it mattered. Grief mutates and seeps away, changing ceaselessly.

It would have to be a three-ink print. Red, green, brown. Brown for the parts already dead. She had been watching it die and go on living ever since Christmas. Four flowers now in advanced decay. They had gone one by one, had attained a transparent shrivelled sepia, wondrously veined. Three had fallen from the stalk like discarded clothing, one landing on the soil in the pot, the other two on the table. She left them where they fell and drew them there. The positions were inviolate. It was imperative to record the stages, to catalogue the minutiae of change. The fourth dead flower had never broken loose. It had trailed downwards from the new blooms like bedraggled underwear, falling with them in today's clanging apocalypse.

Three inks would not after all be sufficient for the lithographs. Five perhaps would do, two browns and two greens and a red. The browns were changing and the greens were changing and soon the children would be home from school. She would have to tell them to fix peanut butter sandwiches for themselves. If she left the studio even for five minutes at this critical juncture she would miss colour mutations that might never be seen again.

She painted the fallen cluster in watercolours, the three still-living flowers in streaky red washing into pink washing into white washing into colourless bruise. She painted the dead flower still joined to them, trailing from them like a raffish brown ribbon from a tossed bouquet.

She decided to try oils.

She clipped up a small ready-stretched canvas, painted the cluster again, same relationship of forms, but as three chalices spilling wine and a fourth smashed chalice of brown shards.

The green of the stalk was changing, she could not keep up.

She painted the stolid stump as it burst green and erect from the protruding bulb, she rendered faithfully the crisis point, the many-greened brown-turning bruise, the limp and trailing shaft, the tip oozing sap and damaged flowers.

She was distressed by her slowness and the slowness of the medium. She took fresh paper and charcoal again, drew once more the seasons of the changing stalk: its proud Christmas erection (fresh gift of her lover), energy bursting from the fibrous root ball half visible above the soil; its wintry wilting; its broken tip. She began to listen for the children. She would have to cover the amaryllis, shield them from it.

They would be surprised that their father was not home. He had gone after they left for school, the conference having been called at short notice. Three or four days. They would accept it.

Perhaps her lover would not come now. It was getting late. He would not want to risk being there when the children came. It was better this way, her husband being a good and kind man though not often present. She had decided to stay with him. It was odd that her lover should finally call when it no longer mattered.

She painted the buckled stalk again as a diver with the bends, jack-knifing in agony through aqueous regions far from the sun. She used many greens, the greens of growing and the greens of dying, the greens of dead scum on stagnant water, the green of the lower ocean where it begins to turn black and arctic, the green of mucous growths on forest floors. She invented greens with mixes and washes. Perhaps a hundred greens.

She could not keep up with the changing amaryllis.

One of the fallen flowers was bruising rapidly. She drew a fallen woman weeping. The woman was chalice-shaped, pale as a lily streaked with blood, hollow as a bell without its clapper. Slowly the flower collapsed. The woman moaned.

She decided to begin the first lithograph: *The Fall*. The moment should be recorded now, before it became unrecoverable, obscured and distanced by changes cavorting and multiplying like cancer cells.

She pegged up all the relevant sketches and paintings. They fluttered idly from the clothesline running round her studio. Laundry work, she thought. The day's washes. She wheeled the trolley with its heavy limestone slab into position, she assembled her grease crayons, she began.

She thought: if the children come now, bursting in with ragged energy and baseball bats and such, the print will be ruined. She could not tolerate interruption once she had begun work. She would have to grind the image off the stone and start again. She would have to cover the amaryllis. She would feel exposed, even to their innocent trusting eyes.

The grease pencil made its soft and satisfying sound against the limestone. She would do a line drawing for a black ink first, before the colour washes went in. A black outline, thin and glossy on the ivory paper, as on a bereavement card. Then the faintest wash of green and sepia, dying colours.

If the children came in now she would simply call out to them to make themselves a snack, to go outside and play. It was getting a little late, they should have been in. Really, she should not have begun until she had them settled on their homework. But perhaps they would not be home for an hour or so and she hated to waste time. Perhaps it was a music lesson day, or a baseball practice. Which would delay them.

It was fortunate that her lover had not after all come over. Certainly he should not think that she would be prepared to interrupt a complicated task just because he was available and she alone. He should realize, in fact, that she felt only indifference after all this silent time. The grease crayon made its soothing clicking sound, the black lines glossy on the grey stone. She did wish a little, perhaps, that he had come over – that he would come over – so that she could show that she was not to be interrupted so cavalierly. She would look just slightly irritated, mildly bemused – as though she could not quite remember who he was – and abstractedly send him away.

She finished the drawing and took up a soft cloth and the etching solution, meticulously sponging the ungreased areas. It was exacting work. If her hand came in contact with the stone, if it so much as brushed it lightly, the clarity of the print would suffer, the sensitized surface would register her body oils, muddying the image. If the children arrived at this moment, everything would be ruined. She would have to start over.

It was getting late. As soon as she finished applying the acid wash she would close up the studio and go looking for them. Perhaps they had gone to a friend's house to play. If so, they should have called – although it would be disastrous if she had to stop and pick up the phone right now. It was growing dark. And cold too. Still wintry outside, with snow a distinct possibility. She tried to remember if they had taken their snow jackets that morning. It was a constant hassle in March and April, the children thumbing their noses at winter, getting bronchial infections from not staying warm enough. They should have been home.

If her lover had come she could have sent him out looking for them in his car. Or if her husband were home, he would have taken care of things. A good and gentle man. She was relieved she had not been obliged to deceive him during his absence.

She could not leave the studio until the image was protected from smudge and change, until the blank spaces were all carefully acid-rubbed and the grease drawing erased with Varsol. Even then there was considerable risk in leaving it untended, but with young children what else could she do? The plate would be vulnerable to random impressions from blown dust, from any number of things. She could not afford to let it go dry. Really she should wait until she had inked it and pulled the first print. She might never recapture the exactness of the fall if she had to start over tomorrow. She wanted it safely pressed on paper.

It would constitute the last print, the fifth in the commissioned series, when it was finished. She would have to work backwards, back through the hints of the weakening stalk and the flowers dying one by one. Eventually she would be able to return to the beginning, to things in their first bloom, the amaryllis in its Christmas cellophane. She would call the first print *Creation*. Or perhaps *Nativity*.

He had come to dinner bearing gifts, whisky for his host, the potted amaryllis for his hostess. He was an associate of her husband's.

"My wife," her husband had explained, introducing her, "dabbles in art. I've built her a studio in the basement. She putters around there. Good cook too, as you'll see."

"I see," he said, looking at her. "A painter?"

"Print-maker mostly."

"Indeed?" His eyes were the colour of the rich brown earth that nourishes tropical flowers. "Do you have your own press?"

"A small one. Yes."

"I'd love to see it sometime, if I may."

Certain forces, though they be blind and groping as roots or deep-sea currents, one is aware of instantly. She brushed his hand accidentally as she was passing the beef bourguignon. When she carried the heavy tureen of crab bisque back out to the kitchen, he reached up and touched her lightly under the elbow as though offering support, a solicitous gesture. During dessert, her husband went down to the cellar to bring up more wine and he leaned across the table and ran the tips of his fingers, lightly as a watercolour brush, across her eyebrows and down her nose. He traced the curved line of her lips. Then he cupped her face in his hands.

She finished the acid wash and erased the black drawing with Varsol, invariably a fearful moment, a blank lurching spasm of terror, the stone slab empty and void, stripped of her ordering.

She squeezed a ribbon of ink on to the glass roll-up slab. She always inked the roller as quickly as possible, her wrists snapping jerkily back and forth, her breathing tight. The blank stone always frightened her. Suppose the image never reappeared?

Suppose something had happened to the children? Surely it was rather late, getting dark? As soon as she had pulled one print from the press she would go looking for them. She dampened the stone surface with a wet sponge, rolling the ink across it, breathing more freely as the amaryllis magically reappeared, form plucked from the void.

Telephone.

No doubt the children, but she could not possibly let the ink go dry before she had the slab in the press. If the children were calling then they must be safely at a friend's house. If her lover was calling, it was too late. He could not come round once the children were home. They were old enough to notice these things, to tell.

She wheeled the trolley across to the press, positioned the slab, laid the paper carefully over it, placed the tympan over the paper. She watched the scraper bar glide smoothly across the tympan. The paper received the fall of the amaryllis, the crisis given a safe and permanent shape. She felt strangely weightless, delivered of heavy matters.

She hung the print up to dry and answered the importunate telephone.

"Mother, are you all right? I've been calling and calling."

"I couldn't answer it, Suzy. I was making a print. You should be home. I've been so worried. It's getting dark."

"It's daylight here."

Not as late as she had thought then. "Where are you?"

"Are you all right, Mother?"

"Of course, dear. Where are you?"

"I'm still in France. Summer school doesn't finish for three weeks yet. Listen, are you *sure* you're all right?"

Summer school? Winter already gone, after all. Impossible to keep up with so many changes.

"Is Robert with you, Suzy? Are you both at a friend's house?"

And did they have their warm jackets with them? Though if it was summer already....

"Robert? No! Why should he be? Isn't he still in Washington? Has something happened?"

"You're both terribly late. When are you coming home?"

"That's what I'm calling about, Mother. Daddy called to see if I would like to stay with him and Judy in their beach cottage during August. He said he's been trying to check it out with you all week, but you never answer the phone. He said you finally answered this morning and sounded very strange. He thought I should know. Is something the matter?"

"No, no. Just ... so many changes you know. Like cancer in my breathing."

"Cancer!!"

"A figure of speech, Suzy."

"I must say, Mother, you sound a little out of it. I think I should stay with you as planned. Why don't you fly over here and join me for the last few weeks in Paris?"

"No, no. Everything's fine. You know how I lose track of things when I'm working on something. I've been doing an amaryllis and it keeps changing, you know. It's difficult to keep up. Do have a nice summer, darling. Whatever you want to do is fine with me."

She remembered, as she hung up, that it was not she who had a lover, but her husband. Her husband who had left her.

She could not remember who had given her the amaryllis, though it scarcely mattered. She could see a tiny new green shoot, pale as the breath of fishes, thrusting up from the bulb beside the broken stalk. She would move her bed down into the studio, she thought, so that she would miss nothing.

THE BAROQUE ENSEMBLE

A S PETER WILLIAMSON was gently shaking out his wet umbrella in the cloakroom of the university art gallery, he caught sight of one of his students whispering to another young woman. With delicate precision, like a mason dropping his plumb-line (a mason of the artisan variety, a medieval or Renaissance mason), he lowered the loosely furled umbrella into a wooden rack. He could see that the two young women were looking at him furtively, still whispering.

Although he paid scant attention to such banal considerations as popularity, this sort of thing did give him quiet pleasure. That is Professor Williamson, he imagined his student murmuring. To take one of his advanced courses is a spiritual experience. He elevates Pure Mathematics to the level of art.

He hung his coat on a wooden peg and removed his rubber overshoes. Some tasks were difficult to execute in an esthetically pleasing manner. In such instances it was essential to cultivate a dedicated awareness, Buddhist almost, of the singularity of minute actions. He peeled off the rubber skins carefully, as one might peel an apple with a small pearl-handled knife to achieve a fragile but unbroken spiral of rind. He placed the rubbers neatly below his coat. The tide line of slushy snow just above the soles ebbed onto the flagstones.

With only the faintest, certainly indiscernible, tremor of self-consciousness, he walked out of the cloakroom and past the two young women. He did not, as so many of his colleagues would have done, acknowledge his student with any of those fawning mannerisms such as a nod or a "Good afternoon, Miss Marshall." He did not pander to that sort of thing.

The students were attractive in that particular way of clever undergraduate girls: fresh skin, shining straight hair, breasts modestly taut under sweaters.

Professor Williamson, he imagined his student whispering in thrilled awe, never comes to student parties or anything of *that* nature. He maintains a high failure rate, considers an A as rare as incunabula, and yet there is a waiting list to get into his courses. It is said to be a compliment of the highest order if he politely ignores you in public.

Yes, he thought to himself. Yes: it is excellence that counts. The populist professors, the fraternizers, the politically aspiring, the television talk-show mathematicians, those who wish to be much seen and heard, verily, they have their rewards. He himself preferred the discreet approbation of the discerning few.

The small auditorium was as yet empty. The concert was not due to start for another half hour and others who had arrived early were browsing through the gallery, their hands clasped behind their backs, their foreheads and mouths puckered as though they had just swallowed something unexpectedly bitter. The creased faces, reflected back from glass frames, announced: I am experiencing the exaltation of art. Peter Williamson disdained these pathetic forms of snobbery.

His deepest pleasures were private and esoteric. He felt for the expectant emptiness of an auditorium prior to a concert the same passionate *frisson* that he felt for a deserted cathedral: hushed wombs throbbing with possibility and mystery, one's inner fire – like an altar lamp – the only reference point, the node of illumination.

He sat in the front row where he could contemplate the props set up for the Baroque Ensemble. It was an arrangement of exquisite simplicity, a trinity, that most satisfying and unifying of mathematical forms. At the apex of the triangle which pointed to the back of the low stage stood the harpsichord. Its chair, like a shy debutante glancing nervously downwards at unsure feet, neatly lined up its front legs with those of the instrument.

The base of the props triangle, parallel to the front of the stage, was an Oriental carpet runner glowing with the authentic pallor of antique wool and threadbare scrollwork. A chair stood at each end of the rug, looking inwards, and a double-faced music stand of the same polished mahogany as the chairs stood between them like a low fulcrum. Peter Williamson breathed deeply and slowly to steady his pulse. The purity of it!

His eyes fondled the harpsichord. There were so many levels of virtuosity contained like pieces of sunlight within the prism of a fine concert. The artisans who crafted the instruments, the composers, the performers, the trained listeners – a symphony of human excellence. The keys of the harpsichord were of oak and ebony, gleaming dully with a patina of reverent use. He trembled to think of all the famous hands that had caressed them, all the guest artists.

He partook, as it were – yes, the verb of sacred communion appealed to him – he partook of the restrained sensuality of the Queen Anne chairs, the intricacy of their needlepointed upholstery, the *milles fleurs* pattern.... A sudden burr snagged the flow of his contemplation. The chairs. They were of the right period but the wrong country. For a concert program of French Baroque music the chairs should have been Louis Quatorze rather than Queen Anne. Something by that court designer, André Charles Boulle. It was a minor detail, perhaps, but in such niceties lay perfection. The Music Department would do well to consider these things. But alas, how many within the academic community still concerned themselves with the rigours of impeccability?

The small auditorium began to fill up. People filed in silently, worshipfully, and waited reverently in their pews. It was, of course, a religious experience. We are the elect, Peter thought. A mystical communion of initiates following unwritten but ineluctable laws. Faculty members and local doctors and lawyers and other professional people adhered to a dress code of quiet elegance. Vests and fob watch-chains. Tailored suits and modish felt hats for the ladies. Students, the novitiate, dressed casually but neatly in jeans and turtlenecks, permissible because the kind of student who would spend a Sunday afternoon listening to chamber music could be expected to graduate to vests and gold timepieces. Everything was as it should be.

He was pleased to see a number – one might even say, a disproportionate number – of his own students in the audience. He recalled having read several years ago (somewhere among those years one cringed to remember) a statement by Eugene McCarthy. "There are only six harpsichordists of note in this country, and they are all voting for me." Something to that effect. While Peter Williamson shrank from the vulgarity of politics, it pleased him that such a politician should exist. A fitting sense of priorities.

He felt that something of a similar order might perhaps be said of himself. He imagined, for example, that an obituary in the university *Gazette* might read: There was always a startling correlation between those students taking Professor Williamson's courses and those taking an interest in the higher arts. This was so widely known that the Art Gallery, the Choral Society, and other such bodies at this university made use of his class registration records as mailing lists. It was said that even among those students who failed his courses there existed a marked statistical probability of concert attendance.

Now the auditorium was almost full. The three musicians entered. After the applause there was a brief eerie interval of tuning, isolated notes fluttering out to the audience like little truce flags. First the harpsichordist, in response to some cosmic tuning fork, or playing to the flawless whorl of an inner Platonic ear, sounded one or two soft notes, then leaned over her keyboard and reached into the rib-cage of her instrument. She had long white fingers which occupied themselves quickly and confidently as a surgeon's with the troubled heartstrings, her head tilted sideways toward the audience, her eyes rapt and attentive. Another note tapped ... her ear to the heart of things – and she pronounced her patient cured with a softly decisive, almost jocular, chord. Her chin and shoulders lunged toward the keys in emphatic congratulation.

This standard having been triumphantly planted, responses floated up from the flanking troops. From lower right the bassoonist, a huge man worthy of his instrument, offered a ghostly "wouf wouf" in bass. The harpsichordist looked at him sharply, disputing with a gentle note. The bassoonist ran caressing hands over wooden and silver curves and protuberances, licking the thin little reed, running his tongue around it in a questing placating way. Peter Williamson found this performance slightly disturbing and flicked his eyes across to the violinist, a blooming girl with porcelain skin whose bow whispered deferentially to the bassoon and the harpsichord, her bowing hand every now and then hovering like a hummingbird over the four fine-tuning adjusters.

This elliptical dialogue of tentative notes, the stating of the hypothesis, was as crisp and clean as a mathematical equation, Peter thought. An uplifting brevity. Ciphers and symbols, baffling to the uninitiated but full of compressed meaning for those who knew the code.

There was a cessation of truce notes, a withdrawal of negotiators, a hush. Then the full panoply of baroque forces advanced gloriously upon the audience with the opening phrases of Leclair's *Triosonate Ré majeur*. Peter Williamson closed his eyes.

He gave himself to the sustaining power of those amazingly long phrases with their convoluted rhythms. It was like a theorem of thrilling density, a piling up of opaque and challenging data. He had perfect faith in Leclair as a mathematician, knew that everything would be resolved with a swift and sudden mastery.

He opened his eyes again to observe how the violinist was coping with Leclair's technical eccentricities, those multiple stops in high positions, the difficult bowing demanded by the rhythm, that peculiar use of the thumb for triple stops. She was managing effortlessly. He drank in the ambrosia of her vitality, the virtuosity of her hand movements, the porcelain translucence of her skin, the soft upper curves of her breasts visible above the black silk décolletage. The moment was almost painful to him. Such wild energy and fragility. So much delicacy. He gripped the arms of his chair to dissipate the intensity of his feelings, to protect himself. The wood was hard and unyielding, an anchor.

Then came the Rameau, loving and restful, a playful interlude between Leclair and the climactic and draining emotions which the Couperin pieces would unleash. Peter Williamson breathed deeply and slowly, gathering his strength, waiting.

There was a brief intermission before the Couperin *ordres*. People whispered to one another, or strolled to the back of the auditorium, or went out into the foyer to smoke. Peter Williamson sat still and gazed steadfastly at the stage the better to be unaware of anyone brash enough to gate-crash his privacy.

Although the discipline of his mind was such that he could counter the unpleasantness of physical proximity at a concert, could almost ignore it, still he had been pleased that the seats on either side of him were left vacant. His soul had stretched in the free space.

And then, suddenly, as people drifted back from the intermission, Ethel sat down beside him.

The air contracted, became gritty and polluted and painful, full of dangerous splinters that slashed his breathing into anarchy.

"Oh Peter!" she said, all her gauche decibels dancing dismayingly. "I just noticed you. Isn't this concert just so very *moving*?"

Like Prometheus he was to be punished in perpetuity for a single act of courage and kindness.

He gave her a small nod and a smile, trying not to look but unable to shield himself entirely from the shocking inappropriateness of her lank hair, the frightening abundance of teeth, the ill-fitting clothing. He averted his eyes quickly from the lake of red lipstick that dispersed itself in radial tributaries toward the hinterlands of her face.

She put her hand on his arm.

"Peter," she whispered, with overloud and pointed confidentiality. He was reminded of medieval fables of the old hag who accosted errant knights, a touchstone of their true worthiness. She always turned out to have supernatural powers which arrowed in destructively on any sham Galahad who snubbed her.

"Peter," she repeated. "Did you notice the way Hymie's face gets all red and puffed up like a heart under cardiac massage?" She giggled in the hysterical snorting manner of a fourth grade schoolgirl who has just had an unimpeded view of the breasts of the schoolteacher bending over her desk.

Of course Peter desperately wanted to escape. He was inhibited by his own image of himself as a gentleman. To extricate himself politely – oh, it could be done – would be not only cowardly but cruel. Well perhaps not cruel. It was difficult to tell with people like Ethel. Their inability to protect themselves from humiliation was so vast and awful that one wondered whether any single specific rejection registered.

"Professor Hyman is a distinguished bassoonist, Ethel," he said soothingly, as he would explain a problem to a math-panicked undergraduate girl. "Do you notice how smoothly and mellowly the notes flow out, in spite of the physical exertion required?"

"Oh yes, oh yes, oh yes," she giggled. "Smoothly. Hymie is a smoothie, a smoothie. A super musician, just super."

Peter, who had never met Professor Michael Hyman socially, and was quite sure Ethel could not have, had a chilling vision of her giggling into someone's ear at the faculty club: Oh Pete is just super at Math, just super.

Ethel, he thought, would certainly cure him forever of any rash impulses of meddling compassion.

How could such a person be explained? he wondered. She could only exist, he felt sure, in academia. She was well over thirty, a research associate in the medical school. Within the small structured world of her laboratory she functioned with brilliance. So he had heard. Outside it, she was more or less incompetent. Not lovably inept, like Einstein. But, as he knew to his cost, totally and most unlovably devoid of appropriate patterns of public behaviour.

Peter had, unfortunately, first noticed her drinking alone in the faculty club one Friday night. He too had been drinking alone, but by choice and with dignity. The woman, on the other hand, had listened avidly at the edges of many conversations, tossing in her voice like a frenetic thrower of quoits searching for some peg, any peg. Always missing.

Was she not aware of the sidelong looks, the grimaces, the snickers, the gradual movings away? Peter Williamson, whose initial embarrassment had given way to a sort of horrified compassion, felt he should communicate some basic truth to her. Not so much to alleviate her truly desperate loneliness, but to spare her – to spare all of them – any future disasters. If he could only intimate that a solitude with the head held high, a lonely dignity, was an admirable and noble thing. If he could only snap her out of that craven garrulousness as an act of mercy....

With considerable courage and a quite stoic denial of personal comfort – he was not given to sullying his solitudes – he raised his glass slightly to her, smiled, and nodded. We people who choose to be alone, the salutation said, have a special code to maintain.

His goodwill and generosity had been crudely betrayed. The poor woman battened on to any crust of human kindness like a scavenger. Her needs were bottomless. She came noisily and unsteadily to his table, clinging to his arm in suffocating gratitude. Perhaps in random compensation for general physical disadvantages, her breasts were large and assertive. They pressed against his arm with a smothering unseemly softness. Peter Williamson was terrified.

He was also of course a gentleman. He attempted rational conversation. Even if her voice, punctuated by breathy giggling, had been less loud and shrill, the enterprise would have been doomed. Edging his arm to safety, he had clambered helplessly around her alarming *non sequiturs*.

"What sort of medical research are you engaged in?" he had asked.

She giggled nervously. "The balls of frogs are very large, you know. Comparatively speaking." She snorted with lewd laughter. "I dissect frogs."

Peter Williamson had thought of children raised by wolves, of people who recover from aneurisms in the brain. Perhaps she could be trained, he thought. Perhaps she could be coaxed into adult life by someone with the patience and unself-consciousness of a saint.

But not by himself. He knew that his own carefully protective solitude could not withstand such an assault. He had eased his act of kindness, gone so madly awry, to a close. He had escaped.

And now here she was again like the Angel of Death, the old hag herself, with a pincer grip on him.

Useless to him now the harmonic genius of Couperin. In the lurid glare of Ethel's proximity he saw and heard only the harsh underside of things: the buzzing rib-cage of the harpsichord; horsehair on catgut; beads of sweat on the violinist's forehead; the bassoonist puffing and snorting like a whale, purple pain at his temples. Peter's own breath hurt him, as though it raked its way into his lungs across broken glass. His mouth was unexpectedly flooded with bile, and the fine flowering of baroque ecstasy seemed rank and lost and gone to seed.

There were some small errors. Fumbled timing. The violinist a fraction off pitch. He seemed to hear the harried and irritable rehearsals, seemed suddenly privy to murky recriminations between the bassoonist and the harpsichordist who was compressing her lips in a hard ugly line. There were red blotches of anxiety on the upper curves of the violinist's breasts.

Ethel's breasts, he was unable to avoid thinking, would bounce and jangle like a lush girl's, obscenely parodic. Her nipples would be cracked and discoloured and would exude the musty smell of bundles of uncatalogued musical scores in archivists' boxes. Or of dismembered frogs preserved in formaldehyde. She would giggle hysterically and lewdly.

He feared, from the constriction in his chest, that he was about to be guilty of some unforgivable incident – an asthma attack, a fainting fit.... Freud fainted in public once, he recalled. In the presence of Jung. And Yeats had been rash in polite company, repenting in poetry. *Now that my ladder's gone....* Ah, Yeats knew all about the dark underpinnings, about *the raving slut who keeps the till.*

Mercifully, in this blind reeling and ravening about through the debris of his mind, Peter Williamson stumbled against the lost ladder, the way out. He had his feet firmly back on the rung of Couperin, sweet genius of order, mathematician *extraordinaire*, orchestrator of the scattered and incoherent parts.

He was restored by the *Passacaille*, he entered the coda, he breathed easily, he applauded. When standing and bravos appeared to be in order, he stood and proffered bravos. He was in fact among the earliest, though not the first, to rise to his feet. Several of his students stood, perhaps in deference to his judgment. Ethel stood and bravoed noisily and shockingly.

Peter Williamson smiled at her warmly (he thought of the widow's mite; he gave what he could spare). He touched her arm lightly, bowed briefly, and escaped.

With all deliberate speed he lost himself among the mazy partitions of the gallery's current exhibition. The lithographs of a German artist, a woman with a respectable if modest international reputation, were featured. All the prints were done in sepia ink on ivory paper. Serene. And yet the content was harsh, the titles savage. *Death and the Old Woman. Woman Raped. Starving Child.* But the twisted sepia bodies (lavishly, lovingly grotesque), the brown curves, the ivory spaces were tranquil.

He felt at peace. The future, classically simple and filled with music, stretched ahead, a long corridor waiting to be computed. Uncluttered. It pleased him that the vault of beckoning days was deserted and private as an empty auditorium before a concert; that other lives were a distant murmur only partly heard.

Only partly and imperfectly heard, the distant murmur

impinged from the far side of the free-standing partition which was the backdrop for *Old Man Stares at Death*. Whispered fragments. A not unpleasant burr of sound. A smudged print of voice from whose centre a sudden embossed detail billowed up into the senses.

"Williamson ... he's so pathetic.... Poor old sod." A male voice.

And then a female one, clever-sounding, sad. The voice of the student who had been in the cloakroom: "... can't help feeling sorry ... so embarrassing, isn't he?... nothing one can really do...."

Peter Williamson remained for some time staring at the earth-coloured harmony of the agonies congealed on ivory paper. He thought of Ethel and Couperin. Of Yeats: *I will lie down where all the ladders start/ In the foul rag-and-bone shop of the heart.*

Eventually he walked to the cloakroom and pulled on his rubber overshoes with exquisite care. An observer, he thought, would have been struck by the singular grace with which he put on his coat and unfurled his umbrella against the sleet.

THE OWL-BANDER

AFTER DUSK, when the owls began thudding into the nets like spent tennis balls, he would take the blanket and the pouch full of tags and wait silently under the trees. Although no possible harm could come to them, other than the elastic lurch of entrapment, some of the birds became mute with terror, and clung to the soft black cotton mesh as though concussed, their huge eyes disbelieving. Others carved up the air with cries like the filing of saws, and objected with outraged wings, so that the nets cavorted like sails flapping loose.

He wondered what a psychologist would make of it. Or one of those management consultants adept at putting mysteries onto graph paper. "A study in crisis behaviours: soothing ruffled feathers in the corporate hierarchy." Or maybe "Tailoring strategies to reaction styles."

Goodbye to all that, thank god.

At present, he supposed, spreading his blanket on the pine needles and sitting hunched, knees hugged to chest, he was in the concussed category. Which meant that this solitary and arcane activity suited him perfectly for the time being.

When he moved along the nets he felt like a god, and drew nothing but sorrow from the feeling. He reached for the birds, gently disentangling their claws, tagging them one by one. How easily it corrupts, he thought; the power to bind and loose. The tiny saw-whet owls quivered in the hollow of his hand, submitting or not submitting – according to intricately imprinted instructions – to the aluminum label manacled around an ankle-bone frail as faith. Date, location, name of the research institution, and the owl-bander's initials. So much extra freight for the little heart thumping against his fingers.

Sometimes the fragility overwhelmed him, especially that of the birds too frightened to struggle. It was futile, perhaps, but he had a ritual of blessing. He would use both hands in an act of solace and hold the tiny body (nothing but feathers and eyes) against his own for a moment. Then he would lift it high above his head, point it away from the net, and shunt it back into slipstreams of freedom.

Though I had the wings of a bird, he would think, I too would still hide behind the night and shun the rest of my species. At least for the present. Probably this would pass.

There were three nets strung across three clearings. Volleyball courts for giants. By the time he had harvested the third net, there would be more birds waiting in the first one. Theoretically he should find some birds already tagged and then notations could be made on a graphed map that was colourful with long curving arrows of hypothesized migratory patterns. Here and there, black pencilled crosses documented the resightings.

This did not concern him. It was not his field. He was strictly a casual employee, having lucked into the work through his second son, a biology student. Secretly he was pleased that he had never found a tagged owl. He wanted to believe in the possibility of defying categorization.

Words came to him from somewhere. *You would play upon me; you would seem to know my stops; you would pluck out the heart of my mystery.*

My condolences, Hamlet, he thought. I know the feeling.

❖❖❖

It was odd the way such lines came to him now as once stock market averages and taxation rulings, obedient to other needs, had come. But perhaps it was merely that his mind, an obsessive retrieval system, was chewing up a new line of software: Shakespeare, poetry, even odder matter, the flotsam of childhood, phrases from scripture, lines of old hymns, the devout *dicta* of his father and his grandfather, strangely fallible as they now seemed to him. With logical corollaries that did not bear close examination: God helps those who help themselves. Prosperity is the sign of God's blessing.

He ran out of tags and had to return to the cabin for another batch and for a thermos of coffee. Night in a pine forest. The darkness did not seem velvet but rough with the risk of day coming too quickly, and only the sharp clean smell of the resin comforted him. In the cabin he boiled water for fresh coffee and transferred a handful of aluminum bands to his pouch. Labels. Name tags.

Cryptoglaux acadica: very small harsh-voiced genus, largely dark brown above and white beneath. Habitat: North America. Colloquially named *saw-whet* because of resemblance of its cry to the sound made in filing a saw.

And what did it do for the owls, this Latin distinction?

He was keeping his own subversive tally of tags never seen again, relieved that odds were overwhelmingly in favour of the instinct for avoidance of pain. Surely the word would spread and this particular saw-whet colony would camp elsewhere next summer? He was heartened by the thought of the baffled biologists, the nets limp and useless as cobwebs in deserted houses.

As a child, Nick, his eldest, had been terrified of cobwebs. Not spiders, just cobwebs. He had run, one morning, right through a web stretching large as a hammock between bushes, and it had folded itself around his face and body like a sticky skin. Screaming and clawing at himself, the boy had raced round and round the house until his father had caught him and he had collapsed with exhausted sobs. Then for weeks there had been nightmares from which Nick would come blundering into his parents' room calling: "Get it off me! Get it off me!"

Poor Nick. The most baffled of them all now. And in a way, perhaps, the most precarious. As though what his father had might be infectious.

He felt a terrible pang of guilt and responsibility, on top of everything else. Letting down the side – always the worst sin. He had said it often enough himself, he who had graphed and analyzed and applied labels and spouted trite inspirational slogans along with the best – or worst – of them.

Cryptoglaux acadica.

Homo nomens. Man the labeller. Josh, his second son, had told him that. For a biology student, Josh knew a lot of peculiar things.

Homo sapiens – though not very, it would seem. *For where shall wisdom be found? And where is the place of understanding?* And where on earth had *that* come from? A Sunday School teacher? Or Grandfather Stewart? *Homo sapiens*, whose memory, while not profound, astonishes.

He had exhausted the sum total of his Latin, but he had the hang of it now and invented a little.

Homo terminus. Redundant man. "Sidelining" was what they called it in the world he once moved in. A whispered word, obscene. By any other name, it would smell as nasty.

Homo ignoramus. I know nothing. Not even what I knew when I started out.

He drank one mug of coffee and poured the rest into his thermos. At his waist, the pouch of metal tags chinked like thirty pieces of silver. But somebody would do it anyway and he tried to make amends to the owls. Avoid small cabins and clearings, he would murmur to them. He walked back to the nets. Beneath his feet the ground was springy as a dance floor with pine needles.

Daylight afflicted him like nausea.

The first week, in clear sunlight, he had seen something horrible: two starlings attacking an owl. Although it was a little larger than the size of both starlings combined, the owl offered no resistance and made no sound, apparently rendered helpless by morning. Of course he had shooed away the smaller birds, but then he had not known what to do with the saw-whet which was gashed in two places. At first he had tried picking it up and launching it toward one of the trees, but it had merely fluttered its wings in a dazed way and drifted back to the ground.

So he had taken it into the cabin and closed the door and darkened the two windows with blankets. After he had applied ointment to its wounds, it sat quietly on a chair back all day and they had watched each other in the soft gloom. He had lit a candle and done some more reading; he had talked quietly to the bird; he had thought a great deal: the blind studying the blind.

That night he carried the bird to a place far from the nets and released it without banding it.

Only on Fridays, the day the pick-up truck arrived with food supplies and newspapers, did he go far afield. His hiking day. Two miles at least, between him and the cabin, seemed required for comfort.

When he returned at dusk, the data for the week (which he would leave in a folder on the table) would be taken. In its place there might be a bulletin from the university's biology department, perhaps some new instructions, and more tags. Also a carton of groceries and the newspapers. The latter he made a practice of avoiding, though sometimes he would turn to the business section much as a tongue insists on exploring the tender surface of gum from which a tooth has been extracted.

Once, though, he had seen his own photograph and since then he had done no more than glance at front-page headlines. As when the tongue touches an exposed nerve and learns a lesson.

One wall of the cabin was lined with bookshelves, most of them filled with biology texts. In the beginning he had read everything the shelves had to say about owls. It was amazing. So much data about 133 subspecies. On the saw-whet alone, a ring binder bulging with Xeroxed articles from scholarly journals.

He could not connect this academic industry with the frightened little things that trembled in the palm of his hand each night. He imagined they would be dumbfounded to know so much about themselves. Yet their scientific name spawned monographs and essays, multiplied itself in encyclopedias, indices, card catalogues; could no doubt be punched into a library computer terminal to summon up a whole screenful of bibliography. Undergraduates whose knowledge of the night was limited to cramming, carousing, and seduction, wrote reams on test papers in response to that strange stimulus, the Latin label.

Cryptoglaux acadica.

What was in a name?

In one sense it had no more to do with its subject than a discarded skin had to do with a snake. Or than *Nick Stewart's Inns*, a disembodied neon cipher flashing on and off around the country like a tangled string of Christmas tree lights, had to do with him. His name like dead cells, shed.

In another sense, a name was as much a part of one as a limb. Even after amputation, its ghost survived. The nerves continued to feel pain in areas that no longer existed.

When, grieved and accusing, the two Nick Stewarts who had gone before him ("called to their reward," as they would have said) appeared under the trees beside the nets, he would search for explanations.

I cannot be faulted, he would say. He could look their ghostly presences, grandfather and father, stern Calvinist mentors, squarely in the eyes. It was his older son, not his forebears, for whom he could find no answers.

It was none of the things you think, he would tell Nick Stewarts I and II. No lapse in clean living or church going. No slacking of enterprise or hard work. Quite the contrary. The problem was, you only had to cope with adversity, with the lure of the uphill battle. That's all you taught me: Onward Christian soldiers, marching as to war. What could you possibly guess of the consequences of being too successful, of going public, of being voted out of office by one's own shareholders?

In his grandfather's time there had been only one Nick

Stewart's Inn, the original split-timber north-woods roadhouse. In his father's day a dozen clones had sprung up along the major highways of the region. Now there were hundreds across the continent, his name multiplying itself like a lunatic photocopier jammed on infinity, a cipher with a life of its own that flourished in stock market quotations, in business headlines, on the contents pages of financial magazines. A living organism run amok, feeding off him like a cancer he had nurtured with his own flesh and blood.

When he thought about this he could understand why his wife would want to divest herself of it, moving out of marriage and chaos and name all in one swoop.

"It's because you won't *do* anything about it," she had sobbed. "You frighten me. I don't recognize you."

And his son, Nick Stewart IV, had put his arm around her shoulders and had spoken quietly to his father, pleading.

"Can't you see what you're doing to us, Dad? It doesn't make sense. Do you think any of us gives a damn about the shareholders' vote? What's a boardroom shuffle compared with some of the things you've faced? How about the time you were a day away from bankruptcy?" His son's eyes were mystified and full of pain. "It's not as though we've lost money. We can go in a new direction. Find a new power base. Show them who the fighters are." As a final reproach he demanded: "What have you always said to me about quitting?"

Poor Shirley. Poor Nick. Especially poor Nick, who had followed the received wisdom of three generations to the letter, overcoming nightmares and bed-wetting and social awkwardness and a wretched nervousness of examinations; picking himself up indefatigably, like the much-battered roadrunner, to reach for the academic and corporate prizes.

After so much allegiance to winning, what right did he have, as a husband and father, to pull out the linchpin? If he could just click a switch inside of himself again. If he could just locate it. It was like groping in the darkness for the button on a circuit-breaker fuse.

The day after Shirley left, Josh had found him mulching the

roses, something he had not done in the decade since their life-style had run to a paid gardener.

"You know that job I had last summer, Dad? Banding owls? My prof's looking for someone again and I'm already committed elsewhere. I just wondered if you'd be interested. If you wanted to get away from things for a while?"

Then he had said, "I'm not worried about you. Nor about Mom. She just doesn't want to interfere with the way you choose to ... reassemble. And it scares her to watch. But I'm worried about Nick. I think when you decide – you know – which direction to go next, it'll be easier for him."

He had looked at Josh in amazement, feeling the same quiver of excitement he had once felt for the acquisition of new real estate.

◇◇◇

There was a janitorial aspect to the work. In the twilight of dawn, when the owls began sidling away into cracks of privacy, the first light in all its cruelty exposed the ground under the nets. Time for ... well, swabbing. Sometimes he felt like a deck-hand, at other times like something more obscene. A death's head. One of those morbid curators of the machinery of human disposal – the man who wipes the axe blade, who sponges off the electric chair afterwards.

He had read somewhere that all human beings, even the bravest and most defiant, foul themselves at the point of execution. A very dirty joke, he thought. A petty and vengeful final catcall of body to soul.

He used a split bamboo rake and pulled it over the grass as gently as if he were furrowing ashes. For this also he had developed a kind of atavistic ritual, mounding the droppings at the west end of the nets, a fresh pile to mark each day, then covering the heaps with leaves. Decent burial. Little cairns to fright and impotence, to that which overwhelms. Sometimes, in spite of the routine nature of the task, he would feel sick. Occasionally he almost vomited.

One of the more lacerating memories that kept pestering him

was a front-page photograph of himself, eyes darkly circled, lips pressed together a little too obviously, his own facial muscles betraying him. Caption: *A downcast Stewart leaving the scene of the coup.*

Like holding up the fouled trousers after an execution.

In the beginning was mere embarrassment, he realized that now. What were people saying over whisky in the private clubs? A banal preoccupation, one he had quickly put behind him. More disorienting was the queasy awareness of loss of power. Not the loss *per se*, actually. The fact that such loss had been inconceivable to him. It was as though a rat with filthy slobbering teeth had gnawed through a sacramental wafer. A blasphemy of rightful order.

But this too had passed and he could no longer identify the nature of his disequilibrium. Each night the quivering owls spoke to his fingers, baffled as he.

He covered their droppings and shook the stray feathers from the nets and fled from morning.

Within the cabin he had two further retreats: sleep, and Josh's books, a motley shelf of leftovers from last summer. He had worked his way down to them after the crash course on owls. They were stacked just above floor level, a lowly adjunct to the official reference library: paperback thrillers (Agatha Christie and John le Carré); also more unexpected volumes: Schumacher's *Small Is Beautiful*, a Complete Works of Shakespeare, *Seven Centuries of Poetry*, Buckminster Fuller. Josh was always like that: eclectic interests. He remembered the boy had taken some arts courses that were not going to count toward his science degree.

"On a cost efficiency basis," he had told his son at the time, "I'm not sure that makes sense. But you never know. These days some very good deals are made at after-opera parties. Cultural polish never hurts, I suppose."

He could not now remember what Josh's response had been.

Working through that bottom bookshelf, he had the slightly furtive sense of reading a private diary.

He had never been aware, with only his memories of hating *Julius Caesar* in high school to guide him, of how addictive the reading of Shakespeare was. His former teachers must have expended considerable thought and effort to have made him dislike this stuff. He took to reading aloud, loving the sound of the declaimed lines rolling around the empty cabin. Especially such passages as the plaint of Richard II. *Come let us sit upon the ground and tell sad stories of the death of kings....* He read *Hamlet* and grieved for his ambitious father and his own indecisiveness and for his brooding son, Nick. He roved through the poetry from Chaucer to Yeats. He understood the Romantics, who cried out like netted owls at the loss of faith.

On a midsummer night he lifted a banded owl from one of the nets. A shock of disbelief, of betrayal even, assailed him. Also a faint indecent ripple of excitement. The bird trembled violently against the bars of his fingers and made the sound of a very old man filing a saw without any hope of the strength to use it.

He tucked the owl inside his jacket to soothe it with his body, and returned to the cabin, his footsteps urgent and nervous as cat paws on the pine-needled ground. In the darkness he stumbled often, feeling his way between trees, and once he put his foot into the burrow of some underground creature and pitched forward. The saw-whet's claws and beak punctured him like stigmata and the gravelly cry emerged muffled, like the sound of his own heart.

Inside the cabin he lit a candle – he could not subject the bird to electricity – and by its glow he waited for the agitated body to grow calm so that he could read the aluminum tag.

"Steady, far traveller," he murmured. "Easy now."

Though the claws gripped his left hand like barbed pincers,

the bird stilled itself and observed him sombrely. He examined the tag.

Date, location, the institution, the bander's initials.

The owl had been banded earlier in the summer, at these very nets, by himself.

He needed to sit down. He placed the owl on a chairback and pulled up a stool opposite it, the table and candle between them. What could it mean? Was the bird incapable of learning from its own history? Did it simply have no memory? Was its instinct for home territory even stronger than its fear of the nets?

Meaning. That was the name of this new craving. Where is the place of understanding?

The owl stared back at him through its mask of inscrutable wisdom. What a sham, he thought. If he closed his hand around its breast feathers again, its panicked heart would give the lie to its face.

A sadness settled over him like a net. After some hesitation he snapped a new link to the existing band, another shackle on the brittle bone, walked out under the pines, and lofted the bird into the black and waiting air.

But when morning came he decided against returning to the cabin immediately. With no particular destination in mind he began to walk in the direction of the light. The pine needles gave off that musky smell of decay and germination.

GOLDEN GIRL

NOW I NOTICE COLOURS much more than before. I think I used to let everything rush by my eyes in a heedless swirl, believing there would always be time for the particular. People too – always there, a blizzard of confetti, a festive out-of-focus backdrop to the event of me. It must have been that way.

It's hard to remember.

I look at photographs of myself taken before it happened and I try to enter the picture, to look out at the photographer. I can rarely recall who it was. It does not matter, I suppose. People liked to take my picture. It gave them pleasure and their pleasure pleased me.

Now that I have dwindled to my eyes, I record the world mercilessly and passionately, seeing it for the first time. I mark each wince and the way a face recomposes itself politely. I note the flash of green and gold in eyes smarting with sudden sun, the blue of winter fingertips, the mottled bloodlessness of a lip bitten with embarrassment. I don't recall noticing any of this before.

I do remember that I used to wake greedily each morning, gulping in the day like a glutton. The sun who adores me, who waits upon me hand and foot, what delectations has he prepared for me this day?

There is a heavy penalty for that sort of thing, of course, though I do not believe I was guilty of *hubris*, being only a child, wildly eager. Epiphanies rode on the clock hands; I

breathed impatience. I loved the way words and ideas dropped
into my mind like rapiers. And I did love being beautiful, I
admit it. I exulted in it. Oh I realize it now, I had more than
my fair share, I was heavily in arrears. The golden girl herself
– a prime case for auditing.

I don't mean I was vain in the ordinary sense, though I was
intolerant of slow thinkers. I never looked in mirrors, except
surreptitiously. I didn't need to. It was the sighing of eyes,
bending my way like grasses before a wind, that sustained me.
I could have lived on admiration, growing slender and translucent, fragile as a moon flower, my pale hair swaying like corn
silk.

She's brilliant too, people whispered.

I would hoard the murmured comments like a lyre-bird lining
its nest with forbidden objects.

I always knew my destiny would be extraordinary.

Shortly after it happened I had a curious vision.

There was fire everywhere, the earth crackling and blackening
like a turkey forgotten in a hot oven, flames snaking along the
ground, wrapping themselves like bracelets around the ankles,
licking the walls of buildings, the bottoms of clouds.

The three of us were there – Christina, Wendy, and myself,
flailing about and screaming.

And then there were the stairs that went both up and down.
We had to choose. Christina ran up, and Wendy and I ran down,
all of us mad for the absence of heat. It is hard to say who
made the better choice. It is hard to be sure that Wendy and
I are lucky to be alive.

They told me I was delirious most of the first few weeks,
but I have had the dream again recently. Several times.

It must be Hallowe'en. I look like the bride of Tutankhamen,
all wrapped in white and driving dead lovers crazy.

The mask itself is the artwork of a medical school famous for its research. For this I am supposed to consider myself lucky, I am supposed to meditate upon the fact that a mere two years ago a case like mine would have been fatal. I am, in a way, becoming fond of my unquestionably distinctive and traffic-stopping headgear. Resting delicately on a neck brace, it encloses my entire head in a stylish arc of glistening plaster, white as a virgin's underwear. (*She hath no loyal knight and true....* No. That way madness lies.) Round black holes suggest the locations of my eyes, nose, and mouth; and radiating downwards in a dazzling display of pleats and folds and overlaps, the white bandages guard every nook and cranny.

Of course I am as curious as anyone to know what will hatch from this egg.

I have, you see, been rearranged in the most unexpected of ways. I am told that layers of skin like Kleenex tissues have been taken from my thighs and buttocks and stitched to my forehead, cheeks, ears, chin. I cannot imagine how this was done, nor what the end product will be, but I can vouch for the details. This is how I obtained them from the surgeons who reconstructed me like a jigsaw puzzle:

In the beginning there was only pain and nausea and hallucination. On the seventh or perhaps seven hundredth day, faces floated from the void.

"Let there be form," I said to a recurrent pair of eyes. "And conversation."

The eyes seemed startled and excited. "Who are you?" I asked them.

They were crying with that stupid happiness of people who are winning television game shows.

"Young lady, you are remarkable, quite remarkable. It makes one humble ... to have saved the brain.... It would have been such a waste, such criminal waste.... Progressing very nicely, very nicely indeed. You will pull through."

"What shall I pull through, doctor?"

"I mean ... you will pick up the threads of your life again.

And Dr. Norris also has done, I can assure you, an excellent job. The scarring will be minimal – I mean, given the extent of the damage."

"I see. What damage is this?"

"Ah," he said nervously, patting the bed. "Ah ... I think you are ready to talk with Dr. Simon."

"And who is Dr. Simon?"

"He will help you to handle these things. He will answer your questions. But thank God the mind is safe. That is the main thing. The rest ... such a mind will cope with the rest."

I don't let go so easily. I made all of them answer to me. How do you mean, repairing my face? What was it like without skin? How did you know what I looked like? Did you work from a photograph? How do I know if I am still me? What do my thighs look like, so gallantly doffing their cloak of flesh to cover my cheeks?

Did you put my dimples back?

Are my eyebrows there?

I think, when one has been singled out in this extraordinary fashion, one can only be analytical. I should, however, confess that I have irrational moments. The first time I saw myself in a mirror was one of these. It was the disproportion my new headgear gave me that shocked me, the esthetic jarring. I mean, it is a natural law that the head should be only one-seventh of body size, and a human body which violates this principle can only be called treacherous.

I behaved very badly – so I am told – and had to be sedated, a pleasing experience. This is what happens: a warm wave, golden green, wells up like love from the floor and washes me right to the cave of safety. I slid back into my dreams.

Wendy came to visit one day. It is difficult to say when it was, time swimming about me the way it does now. After several weeks? A month? Three months? Longer than that? She was terribly nervous, unwilling to meet my eyes.

"You look good," I said.

It seemed to embarrass her, and she turned away as though insulted or wounded. Apologetically she murmured: "It was mainly my hands and arms."

"When do your bandages come off?"

"I don't know. I don't ... I almost don't want them to come off."

"I know what you mean. But we'll manage, Wen. We'll just have to make long sleeves the in thing. Remember when the three of us decided to wear shirts and men's ties and everyone copied us? And Christina wore that gaudy thing of her father's, four inches wide? I don't think you should have cut your hair so short, though."

Her eyes leaped about the way I have seen rabbits buckle upward when boys are out with their pellet guns.

"So many things I never used to notice," I told her. "Like your jack-rabbit eyes, Wen. And your hair. You know we liked it long. Why did you do that?"

"Cilla, my hair ... my hair, too, you know. Don't you remember?"

A new thought occurred to me, and I reached upward with surprise, forgetting I would feel only the plaster cage.

"Oh, Wen! Mine, too?"

And yet of course I must have known that. Somehow, seeing only the white egg, I hadn't pictured myself hairless within it. This is too much, too much.

"I wish you hadn't told me," I said angrily, accusingly.

"Please, Cilla!" She waved her mummified arms in distress, turning away, mumbling, crying.

"Stop whining. I can't hear you."

"Christina, Christina! Oh, what will we do?"

Always Christina. And Wendy the marionette, her adoring lap-dog. But I was, and am, and ever will be the leader, amen.

"Christina, Christina," she moaned childishly.

Distress is a phenomenon in which I have become inordinately interested. It is fascinating, the sense of drama possessed by the tear ducts. First a moat rings the eyes, a meniscus forms, quivers, hesitates, spills over. In the large, slow-falling, pear-shaped drops trickling down Wendy's face, I could see myself, the chilling, unseeable seer.

"I had a dream about Christina and us," I told her dispassionately. "The world was burning while we fiddled on a staircase...."

"Oh God, Cilla, please! Oh God, oh God...." It began as a moan, and then I watched her sobs curl upward in a plume of hysteria. A nurse had to come in and take her away.

"Poor girl," the nurse said. "They shouldn't have let you two.... It was too soon. She blames herself, of course."

I do not know what she is talking about. Clearly we were all in some accident, though I cannot recall the details, and blame is, in any case, pointless. If Wendy is living with it, however, it will not go away with her bandages.

This is not entirely honest. How dare she claim Christina as her special private loss. Perhaps I am jealous because I cannot cry, I will not mourn.

I was deliberately vicious. After all, Wendy still has the use of her face. I wanted to even the score, to make her lose control. One: one.

I am trying to remember what happened. Fragments of event float by me in sleep, and waking too, like jetsam on a flooded river. I clutch at them, lifebelts, and swim against chaos.

Christina's face, whole for an instant, radiant as gold in a refiner's fire.

And yet, as I try to comprehend, to remember what happened before and after, as I concentrate on her face, seeing her there transfigured, she recedes into the past and I am racing, racing to catch her. We are running along staircases, up and down, feet flying ... subway stairs, so many days of our lives.... Here we are on a particular September morning, both of us late ... running backwards, years into the past....

One could never keep up with Christina. Everything, the seconds and minutes themselves, lured her off into byways and tangents, waylaid her with pleasures, with concerns, with ministrations. The thing about her to be loved and hated was that, quite simply, she had only good impulses. She never stopped to think, never weighed things, never had to. Her actions came out pell-mell and pure.

On the subway stairs that day, a furtive Italian widow, toothless and dressed in black and smelling of garlic, mumbling her rosary, half squatting against the wall, jabbered something at us. A curse perhaps. Careful, was my instant, wary thought. Not uncharitable exactly. Just unwilling to – ah yes, the sudden ripe smell of urine in a puddle below her. As one might have known.

I ran on to the turnstile.

"Quick!" I called. "There's one coming! If we get it, we can be on time after all."

But there, inevitably, was Christina helping the old hag up to the street, hailing a taxi.

"Christina! Really! We *are* running late, you know!"

Pausing, telling the taxi to wait, here she comes breathless and trailing clouds of gorgeous selfconsciousness, as always when caught out doing good.

"Oh, Cilla, can you imagine? The poor thing. The embarrassment! And the discomfort! And she doesn't even speak English. Obviously I'll have to take her home."

"Oh, obviously."

Flushing again. (Was Christina beautiful? Probably not, though one always believed so. A matter of blushes and vivacity, of illusion.)

"But imagine how you'd feel, Cilla!"

"No. Frankly, I can't imagine. It simply isn't a possible situation, peeing in public places."

"Oh, Cilla." Her brows had a way of puckering, not reproachful really, more not quite believing me, not comprehending the less than totally generous.

Now, as I remember this, I hear horns and a shouting taxi driver and a stream of shrill Italian. Christina is off like a wraith of smoke, flames rising from her heels like streamers.

"Christina! Wait! We were at the lake, remember? What happened? I can't remember what happened!"

But she continues running up stairs, ascending in conflagration, transfigured.

◇◇◇

Every day, Dr. Simon asks me: "Do you want to talk about your night terror?"

"I don't have any night terrors," I tell him. "Only that dream I've already told you about. The three of us on the stairs. There's a fire, but it's not frightening."

"The fire doesn't frighten you?"

"No."

"*Something* frightens you every night."

"No," I lie.

"Do you remember what happened?"

"Yes." I am lying again.

"You were very harsh with Wendy. She was deeply upset."

"Wendy hasn't changed."

"Ah. What does that mean, exactly?"

(So transparent, so glib, these counsellors. As if I don't know what he is trying to make me admit.)

"She was always like that. It was impossible not to hurt her feelings. Well, impossible for me not to. Christina of course ... that's different.... And Wendy is the kind of person who can never get enough friendship. Ruthless in her own way. Insatiable. Always tagging along, the third wheel, and Christina indulging her. Now I'll have her in tow forever."

"I don't think so. Wendy is extremely ill."

"Wendy? She was here. She hasn't changed at all."

"She is extremely ill. She believes it was all her fault. She believes you blame her for what happened, though we both know that would be ridiculous."

Entrapment! (What happened? What happened?)

"Of course," I say lightly, haughtily.

"It is probable that you are the only person who can help her."

"I don't see how."

✧✧✧

I am lying about the night terror.

Every evening I silently implore the night nurse to douse me with sufficient sedative so that sleep will rush me on an express ride right through to morning, no stops. Yet I am too proud to ask her, to admit that I am afraid of the dark. And every night there is a derailment somewhere before sunrise.

The ward is black and still as death, and I try desperately not to look out of the window. I push my egg head back against the pillow, forbidding it to turn. But it turns against my will and sees the street where the street lamp burns like a coal against the sky, a devil's eye. My attention is riveted helplessly to it, I cannot turn away. Sheer terror rams through me at high voltage and my body begins to convulse, even the bed goes into spasms. It is impossible to breathe.

The night nurse comes running with medication.

In the morning Dr. Simon begs me once again to confide in him, but the street light is watching. Menacing. Mocking: See my innocuous daytime disguise? Who will believe you?

I am afraid of being thought crazy.

"I don't have night terrors," I tell Dr. Simon. "Only that dream I already told you about."

✧✧✧

The days have grown fins and swim around me in circles. I remember the white dress with blue ribbons that I wore for my eighth birthday party. I remember (is it possible, or do I only remember the retelling?), I remember the day – I was only three years old – when I said yes I would ride in the side-car of my father's old motorcycle, and when he made it roar I was terrified and wouldn't get in. I remember the day my mother grew pale and slumped into tears, wasting away like a snow woman in spring. That was today, I think. And my father blighted with anguish, pretending that all was well. Was that today?

At night the planets collide and give off sparks. Red eyes stare in at windows and bounce off bed covers.

Sometimes the days seem to be braiding themselves over me like smoke plumes, twisting, dizzying.

I have floated willy-nilly on time to this amazing point: I have been discharged. My mother, consumed with tenderness, instead of the night nurse, hovers by me. My father, over breakfast, sighs for what cannot be believed. It is a good thing that I have this heavy responsibility of my parents. Behind the mask, I program myself for action.

I have to see Dr. Simon, whom I tell nothing, twice a week. I am still waiting to see how I will hatch. For months yet I will have to wear my plaster shell, I will actually have to begin university inside it, a newfangled version of the pale lady cursed with isolation:

> *But who hath seen her wave her hand?*
> *Or at the casement seen her stand?*
> *Or is she known in all the land,*
> *The Lady of Shalott?*

Ah well, I have always turned heads.

I will be very fair, they tell me, allergic to sunlight, my skin frail as ancient manuscripts that crumble into ash if touched. Dues to pay: for loving too warmly the hungry touch of young men's hands and of ocean and sun on my golden (though still chaste) flesh, I must get it to a nunnery. I will cloister it with high-necked dresses and long sleeves and wide-brimmed hats. This can be done elegantly. I shall think of myself as Ophelia, pale with doom. I have decided to be mysterious and desirable and infinitely remote. (*I am half sick of shadows, said the Lady of Shalott* ...) I have decided to exist as my own literary commentary. I have decided that I will still be beautiful, though tragic.

To believe otherwise. . . .

I do not know how to believe otherwise – unthinkable as adjusting to a surgical change of gender.

We always meant to enrol together, Christina, Wendy, and I. Medicine, law, and literature. Strange how things turn out. Strange to sign up alone.

Alone. A word that sneaks up on me, causing breathing problems. Words and objects are becoming unreliable, turning unpredictably vicious. Street lamps, for instance.

But I still turn heads. I am not ordinary. No. Never.

Freshmen, freshwomen, and one fresh egg, I joke.

Fortunately they visualize *me*, me as I was, inside the egg. That me and this me: beauty and the beast. They are in awe of me.

She hath no loyal knight and true, the Lady of Shalott, though formerly the boys would follow, tongues lolling, as if I were in heat; the same boys who now stand shocked, coughing with embarrassment, who reach out nervously to shake my hand.

The night terrors have changed since I came home.

I dream that at the witching hour someone comes into my room with surgical scissors. "It's time," a voice says, and I see that I am in an amphitheatre. From the gallery hundreds of people watch, their faces pressed up against my comic little life, as my mask is cut away. My convulsions begin, my breathing goes into arrest.

"Please!" I gasp. "Please, leave it on. I'm used to it. I don't mind it. I *like* it!"

The cutting goes on inexorably until I am hatched.

A roar of laughter jangles from the gallery like doomsday bells, re-echoing and multiplying infinitely, a mirrored corridor of endless sound.

My mother has sobbed to Dr. Simon that I accuse her of laughing at me. I cannot forgive my dreams for spilling over in this improper way, for slopping their mess into other lives.

I tell Dr. Simon nothing.

◇◇◇

Of course it was sheer defiance to use the subway when I could have taken taxis, but that is what I decided to do. I bought my tokens with aggressive nonchalance. I nodded to people with my egg head, I smiled through my mouth hole. Every morning I challenged my life, my bitter enemy: Try to defeat me!

I have made up my mind to be beautiful no matter what I look like. On this point I will not yield.

On the train I read for my philosophy course, an absorbing subject. I have been pondering such questions as fate, and how we shape it after our prevailing whim – as benign, as vicious, as random. I have been pondering democracy and how the subway, the great equalizer, is possibly its leading institution.

This happened one day: a group of schoolboys, half a dozen twelve-year-olds, began snickering at me. That is all. Snickering behind their hands.

If only it had been malicious, a calculated insult. If only I could have sent out in advance wallet photographs of my other self, along with pocket handkerchiefs. . . . If I could have stood like thunder, my frog disguise splitting in two, and said: behold, the princess!

There was no mistaking their guilt, their attempts to stifle the embarrassed spurts of merriment.

At that moment – even as I observed with supernatural clarity the subway map over their heads, the advertisement for H&R Block and for what to do about aching feet, the mole on one boy's ear lobe, the undone muddy shoe-laces of another – at that moment I remembered what had happened. The unbearable banality of it, that I had been hiding with such terror from myself.

The lake, the picnic table, the coals on the barbecue, the steaks that were still not sizzling.

"I think we should swim while we're waiting," Christina had said. "Why is it taking so long, I wonder?"

"Wendy didn't put enough starter fluid on the coals."

Her plaintive voice: "I'm sorry. I was sure I had plenty."

"Well, obviously you didn't. Squirt some more on."

"She can't do that, Cilla. It's dangerous once the coals are smouldering. Anyway, I want to swim."

"The boys will be here and the food won't be ready and we'll just have to admit...."

Wendy pleading: "I'll do it, Cilla. If I stand back, it should be okay, shouldn't it?"

"Nonsense!" Christina the Good inevitably restraining and comforting. "Who cares what the boys say? Let's swim first."

Such a child, Wendy. We were moon and sun to her. She did not shift her gaze from me, still pleading mutely.

Coward! my eyes scorned.

I seem to see it again in slow motion: the jerk of Wendy's arm, the can of starter fluid, and a long crystal arc hissing in below the steaks.

And then there was a great ball of fire, like the plaything of some wanton child-giant, which bounced lightly into the air and swallowed us up.

I remember bellowing like a gored bull at the snickering subway boys. Windows shattered under my outrage. Wheels and tracks beckoned with their hideous promises. All this extravagance I remember with horrid clarity. It was martyrdom I was frantic for. Tragedy. Significance.

"A monster should look monstrous, of course," I told Dr. Simon. "I'm sure I had it coming."

"This is quite an orgy." (How I hate that insufferable therapeutic gentleness!) "The devil incarnate herself."

"That's right. Were you hoping for soap opera? Tears, remorse, throwing myself at Wendy's feet?"

"No. I'm not sure even you could do anything for Wendy now."

I bridled at that. "If I smiled at her and asked her nicely, she would walk into the burning. If I took her hand she could walk right out of her twilight."

"She knows she is alone."

"So?" I said, fighting to breathe. "So? We're both alone. Who can be more alone than a freak locked inside a mask? Nobody even knows what I look like. And that's fine by me. I'll manage."

"And when the mask is removed?"

"I don't think a monster like me should be let loose on the world, do you? Scattering my kisses of death? I think I'll stay veiled. It's safer for all concerned."

"The mask is coming off next week, Cilla. There'll be nowhere to hide."

In the dream the world is on fire, glowing phantasmagoria flickering by me like the tattered frames of an old black-and-white movie. The Italian widow and the boys on the subway are laughing without a sound. Christina is standing transfigured, transparent with flame. Was she beautiful? We always thought so. We took it for granted. (Not in the same way that I am. Was. But just in that way ... people looked at her with pleasure. At me with awe or envy, perhaps. But at Christina with simple pleasure.) There's Wendy, floating in the flames. (Was Wendy beautiful? I never thought about it at all. Wendy was backdrop.)

I seem to have a moment of choice.

Christina has gone already, ascending from sight. Wendy is running earthward.

"Wendy!" I beg. "Wendy! Don't leave me!"

And she takes my hand.

Today was my coming out.

I was afraid of the mirror, not wanting extraneous information. I have made up my mind that I am beautiful, a simple act of will.

My hair has been secretly growing inside its egg, soft as the down on a gestating chicken. I rake my fingers through it and toss it free. This is a different incarnation, a new adventure.

I hold my breath and look in the mirror. A stranger, someone I am just getting to know, stares back. This face, I think bravely, is an *interesting* face. When its eyes flash it will have a kind of aura more potent than before. And yet it is softer. Its scars caress it like ghostly ferns.

I touch them wonderingly, rather proudly.

I am on my way.

I am on my way to see Wendy.

"Don't leave me," I will say. "Dearest Wendy, don't leave me."

And then, I think, we will put our arms around each other.

MOSIE

I GUESS I'VE HEARD EVERYTHING.

"Mosie," she says to me about two weeks ago in her frail little voice that smells of old furniture and nerves, "I need a gun. Do you think one of your boys...?"

She's part of my regulars, I got a lot of them in this building. I've cleaned for them, and ironed, and polished the silver, and sewed their children's and grandchildren's name tags into clothes for summer camp and such. They just about as hardy as me, my regulars. And we all just about as tough as those oaks in Central Park, the ones up along the edge at 110th, get the worst of the city dirt. What I mean is, our kids are grown up, we shed our husbands and all our leaves, we pretty near stripped bare, but we keep on going. These days, though, I got to keep my eye on my regulars, I got to remove the occasional bottle of sherry or Scotch that has been emptied on the quiet. I got to be tactful. And maybe they'll slip me an extra five or ten dollars, ever so casual, as though they don't know what that is, left there under the silver tray, as though they don't know it got any connection with one of my boys getting hold of some more Jack Daniels at a special discount price. (My boys have certain connections.) Live and let live, I say, things all shake out in the end. I couldn't have raised a family on what Columbia University paid me for scrubbing stairwells, now could I?

"Do you think one of your boys...?" she says to me.

My boys have ways, I don't inquire too closely, we all have to survive.

"For self-protection," she says. "An elderly woman can't be too careful after something like . . . you know. . . ."

That incident on the corner of West 112th and Amsterdam is what she means. It wasn't a pretty sight, it even affected me quite bad and I've seen plenty. Still, the way she went on, and she only saw it on the television.

"Oh my god, Mosie!" she says. "Oh my god."

She is trembling like crazy, like she's one of those brown leaves hanging on to the end of a branch in Morningside Park in November and a wind has got hold of her. I have to turn off the iron and hang her cotton petticoat on a chairback. They're thinner than air, those old cotton petticoats of hers, and should have gone to the Goodwill or the St. Vincent de Paul long ago, but then what would her ladyship do? Wear nylon or polyester next to her private skin? Ha. I got me a riddle for all these old Columbia biddies, I like to make them stop and think. Question: What's here forever but gets smaller every year and disappears faster every month? Answer: A Columbia widow's pension.

Listen, I tell them, I'm in the same boat, and mine was nothing to start with. Columbia will always look after you, my late Willy used to say. He loved the place. There's students and professors still send me Christmas cards on account of him. Huh, I used to tell him. Don't talk to me about Columbia, I know what goes on in professors' apartments. Don't tell me about Nobel Prizes and such, I wash their underwear, I know a thing or two. Just hush your mouth, Willy used to say. Columbia give us a good life.

Hah.

What Columbia give me when Willy died was a piece of paper in a frame (special paper, I admit, the kind that looks like it got leprosy or something, all spotty and runny if you hold it up to the light) where it thanks him in Latin for fixing their furnaces for fifty years. I still got that somewhere. Under one of the beds, probably. In a carton. The boys might be able to get something for it, there's all kinds of collectors these days.

So listen, I tell these old biddies, don't talk to me about hard times. I know. But I got to admit, I got my boys to fall back on, and cleaning and ironing and stuff. And what have they got? It's harder for them, I admit it, though they got me to keep an eye on them.

Listen, I say, to cheer them up. It could be a lot worse. If we didn't have good old 388 West 116th, for example, if we didn't have old Ma Columbia for landlord, if we didn't have these rent control goodies. Course, I say, we got to be realistic. There's a whole raft of johnny-come-latelies up there in the business office that's tearing their hair over ancient promises to Columbia widows. They got lawyers in droves up there just looking for ways to ditch old promises. You mark my words, I tell them, one of these days the rents will go right through our peeling eighteen-foot ceilings and we'll all be bag ladies together. So just be thankful, I tell them, for what we got in the here and now.

But that's what I call my shock treatment, and I don't pull it out too often. I seen it backfire. There's occasions I've had to call a doctor. But used right, when one of my regulars is into a little "What's the point of eating or getting dressed?" act, it can work better'n a shot of hooch in their Tetley's.

Well, like I was saying, Mrs. C. Talbot Percy got into quite a state when she saw that business at West 112th on the evening news. "Oh Mosie," she stutters, her teeth clicking like knitting needles. "Only four blocks away. And I was talking to him only this morning. On that very spot," she says. "Oh my god."

Well, I think to myself, you just lucky you didn't pass that very spot at three-thirty this afternoon, like I did. Pieces of skull like busted eggshell all over the place. I'm telling you, I'm glad I'm not the person has to clean it up. But all I do is hang up her cotton petticoats and put a dash of something in a cup of hot tea to calm her down.

It don't work too well, I guess, on this particular occasion.

Don't keep her still. She is prowling around like a tetchy cat
in heat, that jittery-skittery way they have. She opens up the
French windows and leans out over the little bitty iron balcony
that got to be at least as wide as a split fingernail. (Everyone
got one, except me in the basement, and I'm darned if I know
what they for unless to give a leg up to certain people like
my boys in certain operations. I don't inquire too closely.) Well,
she is leaning out over this little bitty shelf and looking down
on the mansion, that's the president of Columbia's place, which
as everyone knows is now emptier than a whorehouse after
a raid. (Didn't used to be. I've cleaned up after a party or two
at that house in my time.) And she covers her face with her
hands and she turns to me and says, "Oh Mosie, where now
the horse and his rider?"

I'm not kidding you. That's exactly what she says, in her
Chaucer-saucer voice (that's what I call it). She says stuff like
that all the time. "Oh Mosie," she'll say, when Mrs. W.W.
Emberson upstairs takes off for Florida each October, "than
longen folk to goon on pilgrimage." (I got to work real hard
not to giggle when that one comes out like clockwork.) And
I'll count to three, and sure enough she'll sigh and say: "C.
Talbot's field, you know, Mosie. Medieval. He read Chaucer."

Yes, ma'am, I'll say, very sombre, he surely did. And I'll shake
my head and say in my cleaning-lady-what-should-have-had-a-
better-life voice: Where now the snows of yesteryear?

"Oh Mosie," she'll say, getting weepy, and she'll take out
the crystal glasses and pour us a little nip each.

But on this occasion, the occasion of the TV newsflash about
old Zeb at West 112th and Amsterdam, it don't work when
I drag out the old yesteryear snows. She just stare at me like
I'm some total stranger that's taken liberties on the subway.
Pinched her or tickled her, or something. It's a really weird
look she give me. And she's walking up and down, up and down,
with her hands over her eyes. "Oh Mosie," she says. "It's not
... not *commensurate*."

What's that in plain English, ma'am? I ask her.

But she's too busy doing her jittery-skittery marathon to answer.

Well, I say, if you ask me, anyone making a fuss about what goes on at Hallowe'en, just asking for trouble.

I'm not saying I approve of all that falderal, don't get me wrong. Hallowe'en is no joke, leastways not right here in the middle of the world, north of 110th and west of Amsterdam. It's not kids' play, it's downright dangerous. But that's the way it is. If you got any sense you stay inside, you turn a blind eye. I never did understand these people got to try to interfere with the way things is. Just asking for trouble, which is what they get.

Old Zebediah, now, I've known for years he's had it coming. Nice old man, but not too smart upstairs. I guess he was born into that newspaper shop on the corner of West 112th and Amsterdam. My Mrs. C. Talbot, and Mrs. W.W. Emberson upstairs, and all my Columbia biddies, they get the *Times* there, and that's where I get my cigarettes and my *Enquirer*. Why you read that trash? old Zeb ask me. Mr. Zebediah, sir, I say, I can take my truth straight, I don't need it prettied up like in the *Times*. Well, Mosie, he laugh, an original is what you are.

My boys warn me Zeb has it coming. Ma, they tell me, you like that old Yid? You better slip him some advice. He's not co-operating.

But somehow, even though he never co-operates, over the years they let him be. He's stubborn, but there's something about him. I think my boys *like* him, to tell you the truth, so you can see there is something about him. Just the same, they use to shake their heads. You should warn him to wise up, they say to me.

So I know, sooner or later, he has it coming. I'm prepared, in a manner of speaking. Just the same, the way it come, even I am shook up. Shook up pretty bad. I'm glad I don't have to clean up after.

People like Mrs. C. Talbot now, or old Zebediah himself, they're innocents. They don't understand the way the world works, which is what education does to you in my opinion. And I seen education at close quarters all my life, up here at Columbia, and I can say this from experience. Education all very well in its place. Education give you more money, get you up and out of the basement apartment, *as long as you got no crisis on your hands.* But come a crisis, come hard times, and give me lack of education every time. Give me my boys, give me my know-how on the way the world works, that's the safest way to live.

Well, Hallowe'en. I guess I've seen everything at Hallowe'en. Round here it's not exactly a time for kids. I open my door one time, there's little R2-D2 and C3PO on my doorstep, and behind them their daddy, Darth Vader, and their mommy Princess Leia. I am just putting bubblegum in their little plastic pumpkins when Darth Vader pulls a gun. Trick or treat, Princess Leia say; where you hide your cash? Well, Princess Leia, I says, it's like this, my boy Charlie and my boy Jake, they usually look after it for me. Shit, Darth Vader say, you Charlie and Jake's ma? Shit, we never knew that.

I never seen anyone leave so fast.

Trick or treat! I called after. I never laughed so hard in my life.

Well Hallowe'en, anything goes, but mostly it's just local boys having fun, dressed up like pirates or cats or fairies-in-drag, breaking a window here and there, slashing a few tires, nothing serious. No one in their right mind pays attention, no one has any sense is going to make a fuss.

But Zeb, now, he was the kind chock-full of certain information, the no use kind, but didn't know nothing about nothing when it counted. So on Hallowe'en, someone plasters his shop with eggs. I mean plasters. (I'm glad I don't have to clean up.) Gobs of yolk like tiger-snot on his windows, puddles of yellow on the newspapers, leaking into some politician's mouth and God knows where else. Well sure, a pain in the ass, but not something anyone who knows anything would make a fuss about.

Zeb now, he saw who did it. Three gorillas, but of course

he knows who they are. Well, they aren't trying to hide, they aren't wearing masks for *disguise*, they aren't cowards for god's sake, what's some fun at Hallowe'en? Hi Zeb, they call, trick or treat? He knows their voices.

And what does he do? He calls the police. I know it's hard to believe. Even my boy Charlie can hardly believe it. That Yid, he says, shaking his head. If they gave out gold medals for dumb stunts...!

That is Zeb's first mistake. And the second is picking a time when Eddie Cottle is on parole. If you got it in for a kid, if you determined to get him into trouble, you don't pick when he's already on parole. You just don't do it. It's not decent. And on top of that, you don't push a kid like Eddie Cottle too close to the brink. He's excitable. Eddie *need* Hallowe'en, his ma say to me. He gets edgy when he's on parole. You'd think they'd give the kid a break.

Ma Cottle's right. A few high jinks, what's the harm? The boys have to let off steam, which is what I've tried to explain to Mrs. C. Talbot about Emberson Jr. upstairs. But that's the thing about people like Zeb and Mrs. C. Talbot. They don't have *give*. It's not their fault. Their minds are so full of education, there's no room for give.

Well, Eddie Cottle's not so great on give either, he always overdid things, he's excitable. An egg for an egg, so to say. That's what I thought of when I see old Zeb's skull dribbling brain-yolk all over the sidewalk. It always did make me feel sick, raw egg. Jesus, I say to my boys on the phone, there's some places I draw the line. Don't worry, Ma, my boys say, we don't care for it no more'n you do, who needs that kind of publicity, that Eddie's way out of line, we're straightening him out.

I should hope so, I say. And that's what I say to Mrs. C. Talbot to cheer her up. Don't work yourself up, I say. There's some kids get out of line at Hallowe'en, but there's others that straighten them out. Just the same, I say, old Zeb, he should've had more sense. Making a fuss over next to nothing.

She puts her hands up to her cheeks like she's trying to stop

something from breaking. Well, I think about saying – just to
jolly her up a bit – I don't come from Mars, you know. I'm just
the lady irons your petticoats.

"Over nothing," she whispers. "Oh Mosie. Over *nothing!*"
And she's shaking again like that leaf in Morningside Park.
And that's when I suddenly realize what really putting ants
in her pants.

Mrs. C. Talbot, ma'am, I say. Don't work yourself into a flap.
That boy just ain't the type. He's a sad case, he's a nasty piece
of work, but he ain't that type.

W.W. Emberson Jr. blow someone away? My boys got a kick
out of that one. Babyface Emberson? they laugh. You're killing
us, Ma! My boys grew up with that kid. In a manner of speaking,
that is. I'm not going to try to tell you old W.W. send his son
to P.S. 187. But when W.W. Jr. weren't at his ritzy East Side
ack-ack-adda-me (that's what my boys call it) or away at his
fancy-pantsy summer camp, he hung around a local joint or
two. That weirdo, my boys always say; that babyface got the
mind of a fox and the courage of a broken-backed worm.

You be careful how you treat that boy, their father (my late
Willy) used to tell them. His daddy's a VIP professor. His daddy's
wrote books on Shakespeare. One day W.W. Jr. have a say in
your jobs around here, you mind your p's and q's.

Don't need no W.W. Jr. or no Shakespeare either to take care
of me, says Charlie. He's mean and he's got no guts, that
babyface, Jake says. A dangerous combination.

You think maybe Mrs. C. Talbot is right? I ask my boys.
You think he's mean and dangerous enough?

Don't make us laugh, Ma, my boys say. He even yellower
than he mean.

She mighty scared, I say, since she went up and complained.
He gives her this look on the stairs. He just shovelling his music
down through her ceiling louder than ever, at busting-your-ear-
drums decibels. He lean on her doorbell every time he pass,
just lean on it, on and on, and she shakes like a leaf.

Yeah, my boys say. That's his style. He'll probably work up
to delivering grocery bags full of shit.

He already done that, I tell them. And guess who has to clean up?

What we tell you? they say. That's his style. But he don't blow people away, give us a break. That ... that ...

Ain't often my boys stuck for a word, but W.W. Jr. do that to people. Did it to his own father.

"Mosie," he says to me one time, back before he died, maybe ten, fifteen years ago, "do you ever lose sleep over your boys?"

Yes sir, I says. I was bringing him lunch in his study, which can do with cleaning and tidying up, but will he let me lay a finger on anything ever? (Don't talk to me about professors' studies. There's pigs live neater.) Yes, sir, I says. I sure do.

"There's no predicting, is there?" he says. "No accounting for it. You think the family, the background, the best schools ... but when it comes down to it, there's no predicting. You know, I took him to his first *Hamlet* when he was six years old. And *The Tempest* when he was seven. You know what he said when I asked him who his favourite character was?"

No sir, I say.

"Caliban," he says. He puts his head in his hands. "*Caliban*, dear God. And what is he becoming, Mosie? He's turning into a ... into a.... It's not to be understood. He's had the best education that money can buy, but ten years from now, I wonder if there'll be anything to choose between your sons and mine?"

Well! I got some strong feelings about insults like that. I don't like to hear my boys mentioned in the same breath as that mean-minded lily-livered kid. But I don't say anything. That's what lack of education gives you – the know-how to say nothing at the right time. What I say is this: I don't know about no Callyban, Professor Emberson, sir, but boys will be boys. They keep you awake nights, but they mostly turn out all right in the end. That fooling around your boy does, it's harmless. Don't get yourself so worked up.

"Bless you, Mosie," he says. "I hope you're right."

And to tell you the truth, though I never did care for W.W. Jr., I do think he's harmless. And that's what I tell Mrs. C. Talbot. I do think he's nothing to make a fuss over. What do you mean, you think you'll go mad? I says to her. What are you talking about? I'm polishing her silver and she's got her head down on her book, the Emily Dickinson one (she must have read it a thousand times), she's beating her forehead against the book. "I think I shall go mad," she says. "Sometimes, Mosie, I feel so strongly about him, I feel so angry, I actually believe I could do him harm."

What you talking about? I ask.

"The noise," she says. "It's driving me mad. It *inhabits* me."

Oh, I says, they doing road work on Amsterdam, another day or so, that's all.

"No, no," she says. "Not that. That's nothing, that's background sound. I mean the music."

Music? What music? I ask her. I mean, there's a lot of competition round these parts. To hear any one sound in particular you got to concentrate real hard. I concentrate, and then I hear that W.W. Jr. making very free with his stereo, his mother's stereo if we going to be exact about this. Very good speakers too, quadraphonic, bought at super-duper discount from my boys who can lay their hands every time on the best of equipment. The taste of W.W. Jr. run to heavy metal rock, which is not the taste of Mrs. C. Talbot, no sir, no more'n of W.W. Jr.'s ma, but Mrs. W.W. away down in the Florida sun at this moment.

That music is bothering you, ma'am? I says to Mrs. C. Talbot.

"*Bothering* me, Mosie! It's like living in a courtyard of hell, there's no escape. I am really beginning to be afraid I shall either go mad, or do something violent."

I can see she mean it. People like Mrs. C. Talbot, they're not very adaptable. You and me, are we going to make a fuss over someone's stereo? But Mrs. C. Talbot and Zeb, people like that, they can work themselves up into a state over the most amazing little things. They can't help themselves. They got no sense at all when to leave well enough alone. I could've told Mrs. C. Talbot – I *did* tell her, but you think she listens to me when she's in a state like that? – that it weren't a good idea to go up and ask W.W. Jr. to turn his equipment down, no more'n it make sense to call the police because a couple of kids play a Hallowe'en trick with eggs. I told her: Spare yourself the agony. Because you wouldn't believe the state she got in just to walk upstairs and knock on his door and ask her silly question in her silly nervous-polite voice – which just exactly the kind of voice going to make W.W. Jr. dig his heels in. I told her all that. Just wait a few months, I told her, till his mother's back from Florida.

See, W.W. Jr. house-sit for his ma, but come spring Mrs. W.W. shut up her condo in Florida and return to the city, and W.W. Jr. go back to his live-in pad at that ritzy-schnitzy country club where he teach golf and tennis to rich housewives who also lonely. Stud-in-residence is what my boys call him. They bartend at the club, what they call their up-front business, they seen a thing or two. But their father was right about one thing, W.W. Jr. did have a say in those jobs which he line up for my boys in return for certain concessions.

So anyway, wait for the spring, I say to Mrs. C. Talbot, when W.W. Jr. move out again.

"The *spring*!" she says, like it was a life sentence instead of a few months away.

People like Mrs. C. Talbot and old Zeb, they don't have *give*. They get a little strange, they get wild. They get like that Bernie Goetz fellow on the subway, I seen it happen before. You notice it's always people with education? So when she asks me, after she sees the remains of old Zeb on the evening news, when she asks for a gun, I think to myself: Here's another one gone round the bend.

"For protection," she says. But I know. I see the way she shakes when W.W. Jr. come up the stairs, I see her with her eye to the keyhole. "I shouldn't have gone upstairs," she says. "I shouldn't have asked him to turn down the volume." Well, I says, I did warn you. People shouldn't make a fuss over nothing. But just the same, that babyface ain't the type, my boys agree.

"I need a gun," she says. "I don't feel safe."

So I watch her watching him through the keyhole and then I know. Here's another one, I think. And guess who'll have to clean up? My boys are making a book on it, but I don't think it's proper to make money out of something like that. I'm not placing my bet, I tell them. There's some things, I draw the line. Still, if I didn't have my conscience, I could tell them: three to one says she'll let him walk right on past her door up the stairs, and after that I'll hear the shot. A total waste, I could tell her. You not going to make a W.W. Jr. lose any sleep because an old friend of his ma does an inside-out Bernie Goetz. But what good would it do? You think she'd listen to me?

"Where now the horse and his rider?" she'd say. That's all the sense I'd get out of her. "Than longen folk to goon on pilgrimages," she'd say. Something like that.

I guess I've heard just about everything.

So goon then, is what I say. Goon on your pilgrimage. I wash my hands. Nobody listens to me.

And guess who going to have to clean up?

PORT AFTER PORT,
THE SAME BAGGAGE

O NE WOULDN'T HAVE EXPECTED daughters in full free flight
to be so reactionary, Doris Mortimer thought. Yet there
it was. The world was riddled with a lack of probity, double
standards thick as dandelions in even the best-weeded lives.

But Mother, her daughters said, you know nothing about the
predatory habits of men. And travelling alone, well, it's like
an advertisement. You'll be fair game.

Doris knew that they meant: You need a man to go with
you, to protect you from other men; you can't manage alone.
But of course they couldn't come right out and say this, since
it flew in the face of all their principles. She had to smile at
their malaise.

You've led such a sheltered life, they said. You're so innocent
and trusting.

Which is why you should stand up and cheer, Doris countered.
Better, surely, to bloom so unseasonably late than never at all.

But both of her daughters were against the scheme from the
start. They thought of it as a sudden madness brought on by
the recent death of their father. Via elaborate desk phones, they
conferred on her over-reaction. The views of colleagues in Legal
Aid office and university department alike were passed on to
Doris. There was unanimous disapproval of her plan. All the
ex-husbands, with whom the two daughters were on the most
cordial of terms, were brought in to concur.

To no avail.

Doris was quietly stubborn.

But a *cargo* boat! they said. It's perverse. At least, her daughters pleaded, she should go by – she had *earned* – a luxury liner. If only, they cajoled, she would take along her teenage grandchildren, who would –

"No," Doris said.

Doris was fond of her grandchildren. Nevertheless it was her observation that few segments of society were as morally rigid as adolescents. And the first of their engraved absolutes was this: The elderly shall be above reproach.

Doris was tired of being above reproach.

It was not that she had outrageous plans. Not specifically. She did not expect occasions for transgression to flourish in the path of an elderly widow. It was simply that nothing in her life had ever allowed for the errant and indiscreet, and she had a hankering to put herself in the way of temptation. After all, she thought, would St. Augustine's life, or Thomas Merton's, have meant anything at all without a counterpoint of piquant profligacy?

She did not, however, want to cause needless distress. Gillian and Geraldine had sufficient to worry about, and she had always put the family first – something deplored often enough by her daughters. Gillian had even given a paper at a conference on this subject; it was subtitled: "Can our fathers be forgiven?" and had discussed the slow debilitation of years of exemplary wifely support of an otherworldly scholar.

Now that this gentlest and most self-absorbed of pedants had been buried from the university chapel with full academic honours, it was true that Doris felt in some sense free; that she woke each morning to an aura of strangeness, to a part-frightening part-delicious sense of new beginnings. But her freedom seemed to her something at once overwhelmingly sad, quavering with promise, and infinitely private.

She did not, certainly, want to discuss it. She found her daughters' litany to past waste oppressive. Such dicta, she saw, sharpened their sense of purpose and made their own quite different brands of unhappiness worthwhile. She felt almost guilty for tampering with sacrosanct traditions, but the more she tried to settle into the role for which they were convinced she was (alas) destined, the more she toyed with startling subversions and new energies.

So finally she said fretfully: "After a lifetime of kowtowing to your father's needs, do I have to be bullied by my children and grandchildren?"

She knew that this was hitting below the belt. Jabbing them in the soft underbelly of their principles.

Gillian, a psychology professor at a major university, said bravely: "Certainly no one has more of a right to ... to be a little *eccentric* for once. To self-indulge. It's just that. . . ."

"If anything happens to you," Geraldine said lugubriously, "we'll never forgive ourselves."

Geraldine saw terrible things every day in Legal Aid. This did not make for optimism. Doris, who felt contrite because she hadn't disliked her life nearly as much as she felt she should have for her daughters' sake, had tried to join Geraldine's office as a volunteer. She had hoped it would cure her of congenital tranquillity and optimism. But Geraldine wouldn't hear of it.

"Mama," she said. "You've paid your dues. I don't even want you to *know* about some of what goes on."

But Doris was sick and tired of knowing about everything second-hand from books and newspapers and daughters, and when she finally stood on the deck of the cargo boat and waved to them all on the wharf, she had a deep inner certainty that an insurance settlement had never been put to better use.

Everyone came to the wharf. Gillian and Geraldine, and the four grandchildren, and the five former sons-in-law. Actually, only two of them had been sons-in-law, strictly and legally speaking, but in their various seasons Doris had regarded them all as such. She blew kisses and tossed coloured streamers and generally behaved (as one teenage granddaughter remarked to another) in an embarrassing manner. As the boat pulled away and the first of the streamers dipped soggily into the water, she called down to them: "I'm tough as nails, you know."

And her daughters laughed nervously, with tears in their eyes.

Doris sat at the captain's table. One of the pleasures of travelling by cargo boat was the intimacy possible between crew and passengers, of whom there were only four when the *Lord Dalhousie* left the St. Lawrence estuary, its belly full of Saskatchewan grain. Doris waited expectantly for salty tales of philandering in foreign ports, but the officers were disappointingly discreet.

"My little boy," the captain said, "my second one, the twelve-year-old, he's doing computers at school already. Astonishing." He shook his head, not so much in pride, Doris thought, as in bewilderment. "While I was home this time, he showed me a note from his teacher. It said he was ready to be individualized if we'd sign the consent slip. I called the teacher. He said electronic communications is where it's at, and there's no question my son can lock into the fast track if he's individualized now."

Everyone pondered this cryptic future in silence.

"At twelve years of age," the captain said wonderingly.

"I hope you had the sense to say no." Wendell, a passenger, was on assignment for a book, *The Organics of Life*, commissioned by a New York publisher. "There's a lot of evidence coming in on the dangers. Not just eye strain and migraines from the video screen. Radiation risks too, I'm serious. They did tests on the programmers for a major corporation. Punching keys eight hours a day, watching that flickering monitor, I'm telling you, people think the exposure is negligible but it's a lie. A cover-up. I should know, my father's in Digital. You think he wants to broadcast the dangers? Hah. Those tests would make your hair curl. Eczema, dermatitis, hair loss, way above average infertility, all the early signs. Soon even mid-ocean won't be safe."

"Do you have children, Mrs. Mortimer?" the captain asked.

"Two daughters," Doris said.

"How did they – you know – turn out?"

"Well, one became a lawyer, and the other became a college professor."

"Amazing, isn't it?" The captain sighed. "I suppose it all works out." He nodded at her vaguely and smiled, as though she had offered cautious promises and consolation. "It's a bit like planting squash and getting – I don't know – getting melons, isn't it? Of course I'm away for such long stretches. Still" – he raked his fingers through his hair – "I'd planned to take him canoeing. Wilderness trekking, you know? Sort of thing boys are supposed to ... but he's enrolled in computer camp for the summer."

"I intend to show," Wendell announced, "that a simple but physically demanding life is the answer."

"The answer for what?" Doris asked.

"For happiness. For vigour and potency to the very end. For example, look at what you're all drinking. Madness! If you had any idea what coffee and alcohol, either one of them ... how toxic for the system...." He shared his extensive knowledge of herbal teas which cleanse the body without harmful side effects, rose hip especially, of which he had brought along a six-month supply. They would all notice the benefits within days. "I mean, look at you," he said to Doris. "Just like my mother. All pallor and soft flesh."

"I think Mrs. Mortimer is a very attractive lady," the captain said gallantly.

Wendell huddled into himself, sulking. "I'm only trying to be helpful. People don't *care* what they do to their bodies."

Doris saw that, like her daughters, he was pricked constantly by the burden of a proselytizing truth. He was so young. All his muscles and nerves were knotted, the guy wires of crusading righteousness. She thought of massaging the back of his neck with her fingers, the way she used to do when her girls were in high school – if they'd just lost a game, say; or if they hadn't done as well as expected in an exam.

Instead she raised her coffee mug to the captain by way of

thanks for his support. She also agreed to do yoga on deck with Wendell every morning. She found it difficult to shed the habit of instinctive peace-making.

"You should be more assertive," the twins asserted. Or rather, Pam said this, and Pat said: "Pam's right, you know, Doris. You shouldn't let Wendell push you around."

The twins were supposed to be spending the year apart. Their parents, their teachers, and sundry therapists all insisted it was necessary. So Pam had been sent to college in New York and Pat had been packed off to Vermont. But now, as they joked, they were eloping. They had sent a ship's cable to their parents as soon as North America dipped safely below the horizon.

"Just so they won't panic," Pam said.

"And partly," Pat admitted, "to make them sorry for what they did."

"You have to follow your own star, Doris," Pam said. "You shouldn't take up yoga just to please Wendell."

"But I'm happy," Doris said, "for the chance to experience something quite new and different."

By the time they reached the Azores, Doris had mastered two or three elementary yogic contortions and had decided that the lotus position was as inaccessible as her own youth. This Wendell hotly denied.

"It's all in your mindset," he told her. "You're rigid through and through, you're the essence of rigidity. If you *think* limits, there'll *be* limits."

"You know, Wendell," Doris said mildly, as they watched the on-loading of citrus fruits, "I have been your age, but you haven't been mine."

"Just like my mother," he fumed. "A closed mind. You know it all, don't you? Can't tell you anything."

At Lisbon a cable awaited the twins. *We love you*, it said. *Come home and we'll work something out.*

"Hah!" Pam sniffed. "I'll bet. I can just see that therapist leaning over their shoulders and dictating."

"I don't think they've suffered enough yet," Pat agreed.

They sent a reply: *Hitch-hiking across Europe. Will communicate from time to time. Don't worry, everything fine.*

"And stop letting Wendell bully you," they said to Doris in farewell. "He's such a wimp."

They set out for the Pyrenees with backpacks, while the *Lord Dalhousie* off-loaded the Azorean oranges and half of its Canadian grain, and took on a cargo of wine and iron ore.

Doris admired the sheen of sweat on bare muscles. She wondered which of the dock workers beat their wives and which ones took home flowers on occasional impulse. She amused herself by speculating on the ones who might have ended up in Geraldine's Legal Aid office, and the ones who might have passed through Gillian's classes – if she and her family had lived in Portugal. But then of course the girls would have had different names and a different sort of education and different expectations. They wouldn't have been able to get divorces and perhaps wouldn't have wanted to.

She watched some old women moving along the docks as they sold fish from wicker baskets, and thought: And I would have been wearing black for the remainder of my life.

In Morocco, declining Wendell's offer of himself as chaperon, she went ashore and wandered through the bazaar alone.

"You'll be sorry," Wendell warned. "But of course, you can't let go the reins for a moment, can you? Don't blame me if something happens."

Doris felt that she would rather like something to happen.

In the bazaar, she was the only woman who was not moving inside a private and portable tent. It's like a loose shroud, she thought. Perhaps they are buried in it, a garment for all purposes. She could feel male eyes like a film of sweat on her skin. It was strange to be a sexual object at the age of sixty-five. Perhaps it was the way she was dressed – in white linen pants and a long-sleeved white cotton blouse. The outfit had not seemed at all provocative when she packed it.

Smells assaulted her. Camel dung, exotic flowers, rotting vegetables, incense. She felt a quirky elation, and smiled into the startled faces of men. They did not respond. She might have been from the moon, a thought that pleased her. With a sandalled toe, she doodled *yes* in the virgin soil of new experience.

She stopped at an orange-seller's booth. Five, please, she indicated with her fingers, and offered a handful of coins. The merchant took all of her money without comment or expression – by which she knew she had offered more than was necessary – and handed her the oranges. A dilemma. She had expected to receive them in some sort of bag, and the extent of her pampered middle-class Western ignorance embarrassed her. She felt obscurely guilty.

It was difficult to carry five oranges without a container. Only two would fit in her handbag. She made a gesture of wry self-deprecation and handed three oranges back to the merchant. She smiled, as one human being to another, acknowledging the foibles of the species.

He turned his head away and spat forcefully on the ground between two of his wicker baskets. Her eyes widened in surprise and for a few seconds she remained motionless, staring at him. He spat again, this time close to her feet, and raised his right arm to cover his eyes. Warding off an evil presence.

She turned and walked on, under the shade of tamarind trees.

Stares. It was like a brushing of cobwebs, a sensation of being touched, molested, by something physically insubstantial yet malevolent. The whole world was staring. Young men, slim-hipped, the age of her eldest grandson – and of Wendell – stood in groups and pointed. How odd to be watched so intently by such green and blooming youths. She tried to savour the experience, to roll its irony around in her mind, to inhale its bouquet. But it was not the kind of staring that made one feel desirable.

She stopped and looked defiantly at a whispering group.

Directly into their eyes. She would shame them, she would appeal to basic decency. But they did not lower their eyes or give any sign of being disconcerted. Some of them laughed lewdly. Was it possible that an old woman could be deemed to have loose morals because her face was unveiled?

I suppose they would be scandalized, she thought, to know that I am a mother and a grandmother.

It was late in the afternoon – when her feet were aching, her eyes felt scratched with grit, and red dust clung to her like a fine shawl – that she saw Wendell in an alleyway between market stalls. He was engaged in some negotiation with a boy who might have been sixteen or seventeen. The boy's dark curls and face were so beautiful that in any other country Doris would have assumed he was a girl. Fascinated by the androgynous perfection, she stood watching and admiring, and it was several minutes before she realized the nature of the business transaction taking place. Too late. As she turned to go, Wendell sensed a presence and saw her.

She spread her hands in a gesture of helplessness, of innocence of intention. Just an unlucky accident, she telegraphed silently. And in any case, it makes no difference to me. Who am I to make judgments?

She understood, nevertheless, that he had legitimate grounds for hating her at that moment.

She could feel a blush of sorrow on her cheeks. Wendell gave her a look of pure savagery and stormed off between the ragged awnings. And the Arab boy, his deal in ruins, spat in her direction. If I had agreed to Wendell's company? she wondered. She walked slowly back to the wharf, her feet dragging.

Always the same cargoes, she thought wearily, sitting on a crate near a bevy of small fishing boats and peeling one of her oranges. Port after port, the same baggage.

"Well?" Wendell demanded bitterly, materializing behind her. "Satisfied? Not just a food crank, but a pervert too. Who can blame my mother for giving up on me?"

"These oranges are delicious," she said, offering one. "Better than anything we get at home. Just taste."

"Hah. The ostrich strategy. My mother uses it all the time. Hide your head in the sand and the problem will go away. Pretend I'm out with girls and I'll turn out straight in the end."

"Oh Wendell. We all manage as best we can. You, me, your mother. Why don't you sit down here and watch the fishermen with me?"

He scowled, but sat down on the dock and leaned against her crate. "I'm not telling you anything."

"Of course not. There's no need."

Without being aware of it, she began to knead the muscles in the back of his neck, thinking of Gillian and Geraldine. Whenever they came to her mind these days, they came first as fresh-faced little girls. She had to think them up through time to assemble their faces as they looked now, in the present.

"It started in high school," Wendell began.

Capetown, Daar Es Salaam, the Mauritius. She had seen diamonds, gold, cotton, bananas, ferried into the hold and out again. And sailors, she had discovered, really did have a woman in every port. Several women, in fact. Although not, it seemed, the captain, who sent postcards and presents from each stop to wife and children, and especially to the son he had lost in the maze of high technology. Until somewhere – was it Capetown? – when that red sports car drove onto the wharf as the anchors were raised. A young woman got out and waved madly. She had long blonde hair; she had a little boy in her arms. Both were neatly – even expensively – dressed; and such exotic accessories: smiles and tears and smudged mascara, and a fluttering sea-blue scarf as long as the wind.

Doris glanced along the deck. The sailors were tossing boisterously suggestive jokes to the usual ship followers, but no one was returning the wave of the blonde woman with the child.

Surreptitiously, Doris studied the captain. He gazed at the spires of the city beyond the wharf, preoccupied; except, she observed, that the index finger of his right hand, which lay innocently on the railing, was raising and lowering itself in a rhythm that might be construed as a coded message of farewell.

Doris looked at the young woman on the wharf and back at the captain. His gaze did not shift from the spires in the middle distance. The woman waved on, undaunted. The captain's finger rose and fell.

"I think," Doris said finally, "that you should wave back to her properly. Who's going to mind?"

The captain flinched. His eyes implied that she had committed a gross impropriety. Nevertheless, a few seconds later, sheepishly, he did wave to the girl on the dock. A laughing sobbing sound floated up to them, and the girl held her little boy high up in her arms as though to receive a benediction.

"I would like you to know," the captain said awkwardly, as the wharf drifted from sight, "that I provide for the child."

Much later, coming upon Doris alone in the lounge, he said suddenly: "She called him Sailor – isn't that crazy? He loves to watch the ships, she takes him down to the wharf every day."

He opened his wallet and showed her a photograph, the kind taken in booths narrow as telephone boxes, with one slot for coins and another for finished photographs. The three heads were close together – the captain's, the pretty young woman's, and the little boy's.

"He's afraid of me," the captain said sadly. "He cries when I hold him. Already."

Bombay. When they left, Wendell was missing, but a sailor handed Doris a letter.

> Dear Doris,
> They have the right attitude here. Diet, meditation, healing, the spiritual needs, they know it's all organically related. Ideal for finishing my book. I'm leaving you my supply of rose hip tea. (It's in the closet over my bunk.) Keep working

on the lotus position and don't think limits.

You can write to me care of the Bombay YMCA if you want to, but I'm warning you, don't expect answers.

Love, Wendell

And then Cochin. "Jewel of the Arabian Sea," as they were told by the boatman who guided them in between islands green as jade, past the Chinese fishing nets in their hundreds, dipping in and out of the water like the gossamer veils of sea courtesans. Snake boats, with long curled prows and bellies pregnant with copra, shuddered in the *Lord Dalhousie*'s wake, the boatmen resting on their bamboo paddles as they waited for the turbulence to pass.

They glided past Mattancheri, past the fabulous mansions of maharajahs, past the fifteenth-century Jewish synagogue. Past Bolghatty Island where the old Dutch Palace grew mouldy in the monsoons, a dowager empress fallen into soft times. Frangipani trees and marauding jasmine, extravagantly perfumed, sprawled beyond the bounds of gardens long since run amok.

The *Lord Dalhousie* docked at the mainland to take on a cargo of cinnamon and sandalwood.

When the ship itself becomes fragrant, thought Doris, is it possible that life will be the same?

The streets of Cochin were daunting: wide as the tropics, and teeming with cars, buses, bicycles, rickshaws, buffalo carts, pedestrians, cows, pigs; the heat also a tyrannical swaggering presence. Doris realized she should not have come ashore without a hat. She bought a black umbrella – there were no other colours, only black – from a roadside stall. When she opened it for shade, she could see the arabesque of small holes across two membranes, a map of insect exploration.

Vendors beckoned her into their shops, offering cool drinks and exotic English. *Mem sahib is finding unique beauty as nowhere else, isn't it?* they asked. *Certainly she is wanting, she is buying, isn't it?* They courted her. Brasses and sandalwood carvings were brought on cushions, as tribute to a visiting monarch. Swathes of silk were unfurled. The wet heat and the incense that rose thickly from little brass holders made her feel faint. Faces began to merge with their wares, floating upwards. Of course, she thought drowsily. The Indian rope trick! Now she herself seemed to be drifting away from her chair, away from her own feet.

Perhaps she was dreaming. Or sleepwalking.

She was listing leeward from the anarchy of the street of vendors, she was in a maze of back alleyways. A large bird, with draggled feathers that trailed in the gutter slime, was pecking at something rotten. The air was oppressive with the too sweet smell of organic matter decomposing. Doris slipped on something – cow dung – and stumbled against the bird. With a screech it turned and flared its muck-spattered tail into a whiplash of blues and greens. Peacock! Was this a benign dream or a nightmare? The bird's lapis breast heaved with outrage, it fixed Doris with its brilliant blue-black eyes.

She fled, running and stumbling back toward the safe chaos of traffic and vendors, her legs trembling. She needed to sit down. She found a tiny eating place, its two tables covered with dirty oilcloths. For atmosphere: a corona of flies. A waiter came and flicked a rag at the flies so that they dispersed momentarily. She ordered tea. She had learned the word in Bombay: *chai.*

The tea was hot and very sweet and comforting, served in a glass tumbler patterned with circles of cloudy residue. Without feeling in any way disturbed by this, Doris studied the filth with tranquil fascination.

She felt drugged with peace.

Perhaps I am approaching enlightenment, she thought.

"Well!" A voice floated between the flies and the steam of hot tea and curled into her ears. "You *are* a find!" Some sort of vision, Doris thought. A visitation. It sat down opposite her. Its edges, mirage-like, wavered, but it had the appearance of an Edwardian Englishwoman. Hair coiled above an elegant aging face, lace bodice high at the neck, long sleeves, long skirt, parasol. Doris blinked several times, striving to keep her heavy eyes open.

"My dear," the vision said with some concern, "you tourists never learn. You're succumbing to sleeping sickness." The vision wagged an admonishing finger. "Only mad dogs and Englishmen, you know. Come on, I'll take you to my home."

There seemed to be a journey in a rickshaw and then a comfortable wicker chair on a verandah rampant with ferns. An overhead fan was turning, pushing offerings of hot air at Doris.

"I'm Emma," the vision said. "And I must say, you *are* a find. There's always someone of course, never a dearth of guests. Sailors, tourists, hippies, anthropologists, linguists, all kinds. But I can't even remember how long it's been since I talked to someone ... well, of my own age and station, so to speak. I've just sent Agit down to the Queen's Bakery for some little English jam tarts so we can celebrate."

"You *live* here?" Doris asked in drowsy amazement, expecting the dream to float off course before an answer reached her.

"For thirty-five years, my dear. Minus a little spell back in England right after Independence."

Doris leaned forward, trying to concentrate. "But *why?*" she asked. Or tried to ask. She laced her fingers together to keep the dream from trickling away too quickly.

Emma raised her eyebrows in amusement. "Why not?" She stirred her tea reflectively, looking into the gentle whirlpool of its surface, examining reasons not looked at for a very long time. "We did go back in '47. Perhaps I would have stayed if it hadn't been for Teddy. Yes, I suppose I would have, though it's hard to imagine ... cooking for church fêtes, doing the altar flowers once a month, that sort of thing, I suppose." She threw back her head and laughed heartily. "What I've been saved from!"

There was a long silence as they both sipped tea. One's dreams grow stranger with age, Doris thought. More colourful. She watched bright birds peck at berries in the courtyard.

"Yes, it was because of Teddy really...." Emma's voice seemed no louder than the soft humming of the mosquitoes which waited like a restive audience just beyond the lattice work. Lighted coils kept them at bay, coils that glowed like a row of tiny sentry fires around the edges of the verandah. "Teddy's our boy. Our only child. I don't understand why things turned out as they did. Julian was strict, I suppose, but I don't think more than other military fathers...."

What visions will come, Doris thought, when the ship is breathing cinnamon, when sandalwood seeps from its pores.

"Teddy had been away from us, of course," Emma sighed. "In boarding schools. Well, we all did that in those days, sent them back to England. We believed it was for the best. But Teddy, well ... after he was sent down from his school.... I suppose the scandal ... I suppose he wanted to leave it behind. Anyway, he ran away to sea. At least, that's how I like to think of it. A rather romantic thing to do, wasn't it?"

Whisper of spoon against cup; the tea stirred endlessly.

"I came to understand it after Julian died. Being totally alone, I mean." Pause. "I expect that's how it seemed at school, you know.... Of course it wasn't the sort of thing Julian could live with." Another long pause. "I think, once one knows one is absolutely alone, it is so much better to be among strangers. Don't you agree? An alien knows what to expect." Stir, stir. "And one day, you know, down at the wharf" – the voice dropped to a murmur – "I'm bound to bump into Teddy."

Doris sipped peacefully, at rest in her wicker chair.

"Anyway," Emma said brightly, "a pension goes a lot further in India...." but Doris drifted into sleep.

When she woke it was dusk and the yellow flame from an oil lamp threw fantastic shadows across the verandah. What was the smell? Coconut. Coconut oil. She tried to remember where she was.

"The ship!" she cried in alarm, jumping up and overturning the wicker chair. "How long have I been here?"

"You slept for a couple of hours, that's all," Emma said calmly. "When does your ship leave?"

"Tomorrow, I think. Oh thank god, I was afraid I'd. . . ." With a shaking hand, Doris picked up the overturned chair and sat down again. "I'd better get back for the night."

"You could stay here. Anyway, *tiffin* is ready." She called back into the house. "Agit! Bring *tiffin!*"

A young man bearing platters of rice and curry and sweets emerged.

"And now," Emma said. "We can talk."

They spoke of many things as the oil lamps flickered and the perfume of the night-jasmine drifted in and out like fog. From time to time there was the soft thud of a bat hitting the verandah eaves. And whenever Emma laughed – which she did often – a chorus of nearby frogs responded throatily. Antiphonally. Or perhaps in protest.

"Isn't this fun?" Emma demanded. "Just like old times. A regular dinner party. Of course I have guests at least twice a week, usually sailors." She paused. "I don't suppose there's a Teddy on your ship's crew? No. Well, one of these days." She walked over to a hanging basket of ferns and pulled at some straggling fronds. "You know, you could stay on with me for a few weeks. Or months. We could. . . ." She stopped, and when Doris said nothing, added quickly, almost harshly: "Just a passing thought. In fact, where would I put you? There simply isn't room. Agit! Brandy!"

And after the brandy, Emma said briskly: "Now before you go back to your ship, my *pièce de résistance*. I share it with all my guests. Agit! An autorick!"

They lurched their way back through the tumult of the main thoroughfares to a wooden building on low stilts. THEOSOPHICAL HALL, proclaimed a billboard in uneven hand-painted letters.

"She was one of us, more or less," Emma said, pointing to the sign. "Annie Besant, I meant. Couldn't be worn down."

Doris said carefully: "I don't think . . . it's quite my taste, theosophical . . ."

Emma laughed. "The Kathakali dancers use the hall every night. It's a family troupe. Three generations. Absolutely first rate."

In the gloom inside – the power had failed, and a row of oil lamps had been placed along the front of the stage – the dancers were still applying their elaborate facial make-up. The small audience was watching with interest. Perhaps this was part of the performance? There were, it seemed to Doris, peering about in the golden-misted twilight, about fifteen people in the audience. Some Indian families with children. A young tourist couple, probably German. And three sailors. Somewhat to Doris's dismay, Emma immediately introduced herself to the Westerners, conversing with animation and much gesture, hazarding her imperfect French and terrible German, asking the sailors their names and whether there was a Teddy (or an Ed, Eddy, Edward, or Ted) on their crews.

Then the performance began. To the accompaniment of a tabla player and a singer, the dancers, gorgeously costumed and dramatically and fantastically made-up, acted out the great legends of the *Ramayana* and the *Mahabharata*. It was primitive and splendid. Perhaps it was the drum beat, or the incense, or the rhythmic stamping of the dancers' feet, that gave Doris a sharp memory of love-making, that made her grieve with a sudden painful intensity for the presence, the body, of her husband who had slipped through some crack into non-being.

The Indians in the audience began to smile and lean forward eagerly in their seats. Doris could feel Emma touching her, was aware of Emma seizing her hand and whispering urgently: "This is the exciting part. This is where Rama destroys the demon Ravana, and right order prevails again in all the worlds."

She forgot to release Doris's hand.

Ever so slightly, they leaned inwards toward the stage and felt the damp pressure of shoulder against shoulder. It was an accidental and fleeting thing – as a child momentarily reaches for its mother; as lovers make discreet contact in public.

Neither drew back.

They sat there hand in hand in the darkness, waiting for Rama – upholder of right order in the universe – to triumph.

THE BLOODY PAST,
THE WANDERING FUTURE

"**T**HE BLOODY PAST!" my great-grandfather swore. "The interfering bloody past!" He was half stunned with incredulity and whiskey, not so far gone as to damage the crisp Oxford edges of his vowels, but enough to make him grateful for the embankment railings. He leaned against them and pushed the matted bougainvillea furiously aside as though slamming a door. He made a fist and brandished it. *Litera scripta manet*, his fist said. (After two drinks he sweated Latin, and he'd had whiskey for breakfast as usual.) "It was the Grammar School money, wasn't it? That's how you traced me. From those bloody remittance cheques! Isn't that so?"

"Yes," the young man (my Grandfather Turner) said simply. Most of his eighteen years he had been rehearsing this moment. He stood waiting for his life to change irrevocably. Certain details he never forgot: the muddled alcoholic stink of his father's black gown, the runnels of sweat leaking out from under the preposterous wig (now slightly askew), the cascade of damp legal curls dripping onto the starched collar. Ever after, he could not so much as catch sight of a barrister or a Queen's Counsel without feeling this same lurching of the earth beneath his feet.

As for my great-grandfather, the drunken barrister, I suppose that visions of the Eastbourne Pier and his wife's face, and the English Channel back of both, must have flooded his memory with the suddenness of aneurisms bursting. He actually moaned and put a hand to his forehead, though all he could see, between the railings and the bougainvillea, was the Brisbane River winding its slow unhistorical way to the sea.

In a matter of weeks that same river, in that same torpid fin-de-siecle January, would astound my great-grandfather and several thousand other people, hurling itself down like a dingo on the little fold of Brisbane, laying waste much of the city and drowning my great-grandfather and the interfering past as deeply as he ever could have wished.

But on the day of which I speak, a few weeks before the flood, there was a moment when he hesitated before that past as before a door opened in a dark alley. He stared at the son who had come halfway around the world to find him. Seconds, maybe whole minutes, ticked by in the swooning air.

"What is it you want?" he asked at last.

My grandfather was not able to answer this question with words, though years later he wished he had asked why. Simply: *Why?* Then again, he was often relieved he had not.

Beads of perspiration gleamed on the barrister's eyebrows and hung in dewdrops from the tips of his juridical curls. He straightened his spine against the embankment railings and stared, puzzled, into the crimson throats of the bougainvillea. He made a large, vague, sweeping gesture of disbelief. "This too may pass," he said. His gesture took in the splendid colonial Court House, the unpaved street, the slatternly river, the heat. Even in the face of absurdity, his gesture implied, a gentleman – especially a decaying gentleman – must never lose his composure.

"I should think we are in agreement," he said courteously, "that this was a mistake."

Then he nodded politely and walked away, the black gown lifting and dipping like damp wings.

My grandfather had to lean against the railings and the bougainvillea. He stood and watched until there was no further point in doing so. A few weeks later the spot where he had been standing – so he judged from the newspaper photographs – was covered with fifteen feet of warm mud and raging water. My grandfather fancied, in retrospect, that he had known, had had a precognitive glimpse of chaos. But he had blinked it away and turned round and gone back to Melbourne. He was in a hurry. He was, in fact, in such urgent need of a new purpose for his life that almost immediately he set about becoming the kind of patriarch he had fantasized he would find: scholarly, devoted to the family, touched by tragedy. He did not wait for the boat back to England. He married and put out roots right there where he was, begetting sons and daughters.

And in Brisbane, if my great-grandfather had second thoughts, the river left no record of it.

My visitants. At certain seasons they catch me unawares: when return passages are booked, when passports must be renewed. I wake, sometimes, in the middle of the night, heart pounding, and listen to the seconds changing places, a dizzy quadrille.

This summer, my son turns eighteen. (My great-grandfather laughs his whiskey laugh. *You too*, he says, with a polite but sardonic smile, *you too will pass*. His consonants cut like crystal, his vowels are solid sterling, pure cashmere. *You are losing your Australian accent*, he comments, pursing his lips. *Not that your present accent – whatever it is – is any improvement*.)

He says: *I was the age that you are now, and my son was the age of your son, when the river threw its tantrum.*

I am as far from Brisbane as it is possible – *sub luna* – to be, though I expect, in this summer of my son's eighteenth birthday, to lean against the bougainvillea again and stare at the river. When I myself was eighteen I stood there often enough, a moony undergraduate, waiting for the university bus, reading the river, listening for the future that would sweep me off my feet.

Who will unravel the routes and reasons of my nomadic life? – though they are no more convoluted, I suppose, than the reasons which led my great-grandfather to abandon, overnight, a wife and young son and a respectable law practice in Eastbourne, that most proper of English cities.

◇◇◇

From the window above my desk I gaze out, bemused, at the river – the St. Lawrence River. Down at the bottom of my yard, it sucks away at the base of our cliffs: plucks and thaws, plucks and thaws. I live at the desiccating edge of things, on the dividing line between two countries, nowhere.

My grandfather's face, pensive, hangs in the maples like a moon. *Never*, he begs, *never live on the banks of a river.*

This is very high ground, I assure him. *Sixty feet of limestone between me and the water.*

My great-grandfather comes lurching through the trees, avoiding his son. He laughs his well-bred English laugh. He laughs his turn-of-the-century Brisbane tavern laugh. *This too will pass*, he promises.

◇◇◇

After the Second World War, when my father came home from the Air Force, jobs were not so easy to come by in Melbourne. Too many returning soldiers and new immigrants from Europe, I suppose. When an offer of work came from Brisbane there was no question about whether we would go, though neighbors and relations, stunned, all said: "Brisbane! You can't be serious?"

"When you buy a house," warned my grandfather, "buy on high ground, and well away from the river."

But memory is short. In Brisbane my grandfather's advice was thought to be quaint and neurotic. Just the same, my father would not look at a house near the river, nor one that was not on high ground. He had cause to be grateful in Christmas '74 when the river got up to its old tricks, thrashing around like a dragon in fitful sleep.

"There's a purpose behind everything," my father told me

by trans-Pacific phone call on the morning following the disaster. My father is a deeply religious man. "Sometimes we have to wait a long time, almost a century in fact, to know what was in the mind of God."

"Dad," I say awkwardly. My father and I have, for a long time now, avoided discussing many topics, especially such matters as what may be on the mind of God. "Everyone's safe, then?"

"Hardly everyone," he says with a hint of reproach. "But your parents and your brothers and their families are safe. We're all pitching in with the relief work, everyone is, it's fantastic. I thought you'd want to know we're okay, in case you saw something on the news." Then he laughs, self-deprecatingly: "Though I don't suppose Brisbane . . . over there. I suppose we don't count for too much in the big wide world." There is a silence and then he laughs again. "If you could see me! Mud from head to toe. But it isn't funny. It's awful, it's tragic seeing them crammed into schools and churches. They look so dazed."

"Dad . . . " I say, but am awash in old places, my old schools, the university bus stop, the park on the river bank where I had my first kiss.

"The water's receding now," my father says. "The worst's over. But it'll be *days* . . . and the *mud*! Heaven knows how long before the mud will be cleared away. I wonder if Brisbane will ever look the same again. I wonder if anyone will stay."

People do stay, of course.

They even – amazing as it seems – build right on the river bank again.

As for us, for my expatriate husband and myself, the mere thought of Brisbane almost ceasing to be did something to us. We couldn't afford it, but we had to go home – come home – that summer; the *northern* summer, that is – though it was a mild and sweet-smelling winter in Brisbane, and the wattles were in bloom along the river.

❖❖❖

"Since 'ow long 'ave you been in Canada?" asks the telephone voice from the Australian High Commission in Ottawa. It is a French Canadian voice, heavily accented, but I long ago gave up expecting the logical in matters such as this.

"Much longer than I expected," I answer.

"Why did you come?"

"Academic reasons." In both senses, I think. "It wasn't planned, really. It just arrived."

"*Il est arrivé?*" she says, thrown slightly off course.

"*C'est ca. Exactement,*" I assure her. "Look, is this relevant to the renewal of my Australian passport?"

"Yes," she says. "Why do you stay 'ere?"

"Stahier?"

"*Au Canada.*"

"Ah. For the same academic reasons. I really can't see what this has to. . . ."

"Before we can renew your Australian passport," she explains . . . (and I puzzle over that plural. Who is this French Canadian Australian *we?*) . . . "Before we can renew, you 'ave to sign a document authorizing us to conduct a search of Canadian immigration files. As long as you 'ave never applied for Canadian citizenship, there is *pas de problème.*"

"How nice," I say, cut to the quick. And hear my great-grandfather's laugh.

◇◇◇

Television had just come to Brisbane in 1953, though no families we knew could afford a set. For the coronation, we loaded folding chairs into family cars and drove into the city and sat outside shop windows to watch as Her Majesty arrived at Westminster Abbey. It was all very festive.

I remember the backyard parties, the fireworks, the decorations. Ours were splendid, especially on the garage, a corrugated-iron structure that slumped against the banana clump. A mango tree leaned over its rotting wooden doors, which we had festooned – my brothers and I – with red, white, and blue; with the Royal Ensign, the Union Jack, the Southern Cross. ELIZABETH REGINA, in huge wobbley letters, pricked its way across the undulating wall. Below this, stretching all the way from the mango tree to the banana palms, was a long accordion-pleated poster (we had all been given them in school) of the Royal Coach and the horses and the footmen and the Crown Jewels and each item of the coronation regalia, especially that part of the royal hemline where the Golden Wattle was embroidered.

"Magnificent!" my father said.

He was, I recall, deeply moved, perhaps by the ingenuity and acrobatic skill that had been involved in climbing the mango tree and springing across to the garage roof in order to hang the bunting. He put his hand on my shoulder. He never held it against me (not even, I truly believe, in secret) that I, his firstborn, was a daughter. "Tradition." he said, and I was both curious and embarrassed about the huskiness in his voice. "We have to know where we come from. My own father and grandfather. . . ."

He went astray in his thoughts and I had to prompt him.

"Did Grandpa ever see the old king?"

"He saw the old *Queen* once, Victoria. He was very young, it was before his father . . . Your great-grandfather, I'm afraid, was a scoundrel, but still, even he . . . . There was money that kept coming for your grandfather to go to Grammar School. All those years when nobody knew where . . . so even he had a sense of . . ."

There was a long silence.

"Well, anyway, now we belong here," he said. "*Here.*" He looked at our little wooden house, and the rusty iron garage, and the gravel tracks of the driveway, and the old Bedford van and the mango tree and the passionfruit vines hanging matted over the fences. He took a deep princely breath of that damp and heavy air, and I remember thinking with a thrill of proprietary power: How *rich* we are!

"This is the place where we belong," he said. "You'll always belong here. And your children. And your children's children."

About me, I think, he was right. But perhaps it was only to be expected that I would be nomadic. Perhaps it was in my blood.

◇◇◇

My son and I are walking beside the Charles River in Cambridge, Massachusetts, because – for the time being – I am teaching at M.I.T.

"Well," he says, "I've decided on the University of Toronto."

"I'm glad," I tell him. "I'm glad we'll still all be living in the same country. Well," I correct myself sheepishly, gesturing at Boston. "Most of the time, that is."

My son shrugs and grins at me. He finds me unnecessarily anxious about separations. Movement is the norm of his life.

My son seems to me very American. That is to say, unlike me, he has an easy confidence that the world is manageable. He is not unduly bothered by absurdity. The random and irrational do not cause him anxiety. This, it seems to me, is because of his birth and his many subsequent summers in Los Angeles. He seems to me very Californian.

◇◇◇

I have a vivid memory of walking with my Grandfather Turner in the Ballarat Gardens, not far from Melbourne. It was before we move to Brisbane, so I must have been five or six. We must have gone walking in the Gardens quite often because there are several photographs of us – black and white, not too clear – here and there in family collections.

My grandfather does not look in the least like other Australian grandfathers. He wears a tweed suit with a vest and watch chain. He carries an elegant walking stick. He is holding my hand. I am wearing the long golden corkscrew curls which I hate but which everyone else considers adorable. I am also wearing one of the little dresses with smocked bodices which I frequently rip while climbing trees.

The paths of the Ballarat Gardens are lined with statues. My grandfather, who was the school headmaster until he retired, plays a game with me.

"This one?" he asks, pointing with his stick.

"That's Mercury."

"And this one?"

"That's the Venus de Milo."

"And this one?"

"That's Persephone."

"And why is Persephone weeping?"

"She misses . . . I forget her name. She misses her mother."

"Demeter," he says. "She misses her mother Demeter. And she wants to go back. Whichever world she's in, she always misses the other one and wants to go back."

We emerge from the avenue of statues at the shore of the Ballarat Lake. We walk out on the little wooden jetty.

"When I was little," my grandfather says, "about as old as you are now, my father used to take me walking on the Eastbourne Pier. Just like this."

I already know (because with grandfather all conversations are lessons of one kind or another) that Eastbourne is in England and that England is on the other side of the world, a place as easily imagined and as fabulous as Persephone's Underworld. We sit on the end of the jetty and I swing my legs back and forth and throw pebbles in the water.

"Look at the dragonflies," my grandfather says, pointing. But there is something in his voice.

"Grandpa?" I ask curiously. "What's the matter?"

He doesn't answer, but he puts his walking stick carefully down on the jetty, and takes me on his lap and holds me so tightly it hurts.

MORGAN MORGAN

M Y GRANDFATHER, Morgan Morgan, was a yodeller and a breeder of dahlias. On Collins Street and Bourke Street, I could tug at his hand and plead "Please, Grandpa, please!" and he would throw back his head and do something mysterious in his throat and his yodel would unfurl itself like a silk ribbon. All the trams in Melbourne would come to a standstill, entangled. Bewitched pedestrians stopped and stared. But this was nothing compared with former powers: when he was a young man on the goldfields, handsome and down on his luck, the girls for miles around would come running. Yodel-o-o-o, my grandfather would sing, snaring them, winding them in. The girls would sigh and sway like cobras in the strands of his voice. He was a charmer.

"Get along with you, Morg. You're bad for business," Mrs. Blackburn would say. Flowers bloomed by the bucketful around her. She would lean across roses and carnations, she would catch at his sleeve. "Here's a daisy for the Nipper," and she'd tuck it behind my ear. She didn't want him to move on at all, even I knew that. "Your grandpa," she had said to me often enough, "is a fine figure of a man, they don't make men like him anymore." She'd pull one of her carnations from a bucket and swing the stem in her fingers. "A gentleman is a gentleman," she'd sigh. "Even if he is poor as a church mouse and never found a thimbleful of gold."

It was not entirely true, Grandpa told me, that he'd never struck it rich on the goldfields – the *Kalgoorlie* goldfields, he'd say, with a loving hesitation on the *o*'s and *l*'s, a rallentando which intimated that music had gone from the language since The Rush petered out.

In those exotic and demented times, men were obsessed with the calibration of luck. Not Morgan Morgan. While other men mapped out their fevers with calipers, measuring the likely run of a seam from existing strikes, Grandpa Morgan simply watched for the aura. Wherever the aura settled, he panned or dug.

"Crazy as a bandicoot," the publican told him. "You've got to have a *system*, mate!"

But Morgan Morgan knew that gold was a gift, it never came to men of system, never had. "King David danced before the Lord," he pointed out, "which goes to show; and his gold-mines were the richest in the world, I read it somewhere, some archaeologist bloke has proved it." Grandpa had his own methods of fossicking, in scripture or creek bed, it was all the same to him. He found what he wanted, or at any rate learned to want what he found.

He labored at strings of waterholes that were known to be panned out. He was after the Morgan Nugget. This was how it appeared to him in a vision: as big as a man's fist, blackened, gnarled like a prune, cobwebby with the roots of creek ferns. He expected its presence to be announced by an echo of Welsh choirs in the tri-tree and eucalypt scrub. And it was, it was. One day, with the strains of *Cwm Rhondda* all around him, he scratched at a piece of rock with a broken fingernail and the sun caught the gash and almost blinded him.

"Solid gold," he told me. "And big as a man's fist." Not for the first time, he knew himself to be a man of destiny.

"What did you do with it, Grandpa?" I was full of awe. When he spoke of the past, I heard the surf of the delectable world of turbulence that raged beyond our garden wall. We were still at the old place in Ringwood then, across from the

railway station. If I buried my face in the box-hedge of golden
privet, I could hear the rush of Grandpa's life, the trains
careering past to Mitcham and Box Hill and Richmond. He
would listen too, leaning into the sound, and I would see his
eyes travel on beyond Richmond, beyond Footscray even, out
towards the unfenceable Nullarbor Plain and Kalgoorlie.

"What did you do with it, Grandpa?"

"With what?" he would ask from far away.

"With the Morgan Nugget?"

"I put it down again," he said, "right back down where I
found it, inside the vision. It's still waiting just where I put it.
Listen," he said, "if you put your ear to the Morgan Dahlia,
you can hear it waiting."

I buried my ear in those soft salmon ruchings of petals and
heard the deep hush of the past. And then *pop, pop*: he pinched
the calix with his fingers. "That's the sound of the Morgan
Nugget," he said, "when it gets impatient. It's waiting for one
of us to find it again."

"Dad!" Grandma Morgan, with a basket of eggs on her arm,
came down the path from the hen house. "Don't confuse the
child with your nonsense." She lifted her eyebrows at me.
"Always could talk the leg off an iron pot, your Grandpa."

"Pot calling the kettle black, I'd say," he grumbled. He
hated to be listened in on; I hated it too. I didn't like the way
the Morgan history drooped at the edges when other people
were around.

Grandma Morgan was picking mint and tossing the sprigs into her basket. The leaves lay green and vivid against the eggs.
"Came to tell you the pension cheques have arrived," she said.

"Well, praise be," said Grandpa, mollified. "Praise be.
There's corn in Egypt yet. And on top of that," he whispered,
as she moved off towards the house, "the Morgan Nugget's
still waiting."

"Dad! No more nonsense. That child is never going to know
the difference between truth and lies, you mark my words."

"Got eyes in the back of her head," Grandpa grumbled.

"And ears in the wind. No flies on her, no siree."

It was one of his favorite sayings: *No flies on so-and-so, no siree*. To me it implied an opposite state, an unsavory kind of person, stupid, sticky, smelling overly sweet in the manner of plums left on the ground beneath our tree for too long. I imagined this person – the person on whom there *were* flies – to be pale and bloated, and to have bad breath and unwashed socks.

There was a man who delivered bonemeal for the dahlia garden on whom I thought there might be flies – if only one could see him at an unguarded moment. His clothes gave off a rich rancid smell. When he laughed it was like looking into the squishy dark mush of fruit I had to collect from the lawn before a mowing. Those few teeth which the bonemeal man still had – they announced themselves like unvanquished sentinels on a crumbling rampart – were given over to a delicate vegetation. I recognized it: it was the same silky green fur that coated the fallen plums over which floated little black parasols of flies.

Yet one day, when I came out to the dahlia garden just as the bonemeal man was leaving, Grandpa Morgan was tossing his fine head of hair in the wind and laughing his fine Welsh laugh. The bonemeal man was laughing too, trundling his barrow down our path, doubled up with mirth between its shafts, his green teeth waving about like banners.

"Grandpa, what is it, what is it? Why are you laughing, Grandpa?"

"Oh," Grandpa gasped, patting me on the head in the way that meant a subject was not for discussng. "No flies on *him*, no siree."

❖❖❖

This was the best thing: I could always count on Grandpa Morgan to be outrageous. That was the word people used: the neighbors, my grandmother, my mother, my uncles. "He's *outrageous*," they would say, shaking their heads and throwing up their hands and smiling.

If I asked him to, he would yodel in the schoolyard when he came to fetch me, and abracadabra, we two were the hub of a circle of awed envy. When I passed the Teachers' Room at morning tea time, I'd hear the older ones whisper and smile: "That's Morgie's granddaughter."

On our walks he would stop and talk to everyone we met, "to *anyone*, anyone at all," Uncle Cyril would groan. He spoke to the butcher, the baker, the lady in the cake shop, to men who did shady undiscussable things, even men who smelled of horses and *took bets*, whatever that was.

"What can you be thinking of?" Grandma would say, "with the child hearing every word? A man *known* to be mixed up with off-course betting."

I knew bets to be deeply evil. I imagined them to be huge and ravenous and almost hidden behind fearful masks. Once upon a time, in Kalgoorlie, Grandpa himself had made bets, but that was before the Lord saved him and showed him the light. Now, he said, he only bet on the Day of Judgment. Still, he couldn't see any harm in talking to people who "knew horses." He would introduce me. "This is Paddy," he would say; "A man who knows horses if ever anyone did." I myself had no interest in knowing horses on account of their large and alarming teeth, but I rather liked those brave horse-knowing men.

Sometimes Grandma, shocked, would call out: "Dad! I want to have a word with you, Dad." From the front window, she would have watched us coming over the bridge from the Ring-wood Station. The most *interesting* people came off the trains and walked over that bridge. Grandma would have seen us stop and talk to some gentleman who wore string, perhaps, for suspenders, and whose shoes were stuffed in an intricate way with newspapers, and who gave off the rank smell of the pubs. "Dad!" she would say. "What are you *thinking* of, to introduce the child to such strangers?"

"Strangers?" Grandpa would raise his eyebrows in surprise. "That wasn't a stranger. That was Bluey McTavish from back of Geelong. We don't know any strangers."

This was certainly true, though we'd only just met Mr. Bluey McTavish of Geelong, whose life history we would discuss over the sorting of dahlia bulbs. I don't know what it was about Grandpa Morgan, but people told him a great deal about themselves very quickly. "There aren't any such people as strangers," he told me. "Or if there are, I've never met them."

"I don't know what's going to come of that child," Grandma Morgan said, throwing up her hands and trying not to smile. "But one thing's certain: she'll never know the difference between truth and lies."

Grandpa said with ruffled dignity: "One thing she'll know about is dahlias."

The dahlias, the dahlias. They stretched to the edge of the world. When I stood between the rows, I saw nothing but jungle, with great suns of flowers above me, so heavy they nodded on their stalks and shone down through the forests of their own leaves. Such a rainbow of suns: from creamy white to a purple that was almost black. The dahlias believed in excess: they could never have too many petals. The dahlia which could crowd the most pleatings of pure light about its center won a blue ribbon at the Melbourne Show. It was an article of faith with us that some year the Morgan Dahlia would win that ribbon.

Grandpa Morgan did things to the bulbs and the soil. He married broad-petalled pinks to pintucked yellows; he introduced sassy purples to smocked whites with puffed sleeves and lacy hems. He watched over his nurslings, he crooned to them, he prayed. To birds and snails, he issued strong Welsh warnings (the Lord having taken away a certain range of Australian vocabulary). As his flowerlings grew, he murmured endearments; and they gathered themselves up into a delirium of pleats, rank upon rank of petals, tier upon tier, frilled prima donnas. The color of the Morgan dahlia was a salmon that could make judges weep, the salmon of a baby's cheek, the color of a lover's whisper. And it did win yellow ribbons, and red, at the Melbourne Show, but never the coveted blue.

"Is it waiting till we find the Morgan Nugget again?" I asked.

"Very likely," Grandpa said. "Very likely."

❖❖❖

The day Grandma came out with the news of Uncle Charlie, we were deep in dahlias.

"Dad," she said. "Charlie's gone."

Grandpa paused in mid-weeding. A clump of clover and crab-grass dangled from between his fingers. He sank down on the ground between the dahlias and rested his head in his hands. "Well," he said, sadly and slowly. "Charlie. So Charlie went first."

"Where's he gone?" I wanted to know.

"Uncle Charlie's gone to heaven," Grandma told me, and Grandpa said: "He's dead." He pushed his trowel into the soil and lifted up a handful of earth. It was alive with ants and worms, we watched it move in the palm of his hand. "I'm next," he sighed, and he smelled the earth and held it for me to smell, and he rubbed it against his cheek as though it were a kitten. "I'm next, I suppose."

"Next for what?"

"Next for dying," he said.

"What happens when you die, Grandpa?"

"They put you in a box and they bury you under the ground with the dahlia bulbs."

I stared at him in horror. "Uncle Charlie should run away and hide."

"You can't run away when you're dead," he said.

"Grandpa," I whispered, beginning to shiver, "will they do it to you?"

"Yes," he said.

"And to me?"

I crept between his earth-covered arms and he held me tightly and rocked me back and forth between the dahlias. "Yes," he

sighed, "one day, yes. That's the way it is. But then we'll be
with the Lord."

I didn't want to be with the Lord. I had a brilliant idea.
"Grandpa," I said, "we'll run away *before* we die. I know a
very good place in the woodshed, they'd never find us."

"Dad!" Grandma's voice steamed over with exasperation.
"Now just what have you been telling her this time? How will
that child ever know the difference between truth and a lie?
Uncle Charlie," she said to me, "has gone straight to heaven,
and that is the simple truth."

❖❖❖

Mr. Peabody knew the truth. Every Sunday it spoke in his
bones, it shook him from head to foot.

There must have been some obscure and ancient rule at
church. It must have been this rule which forced Mr. Peabody,
week after week, to sit directly in front of Grandpa Morgan.
Mr. Peabody was a tiny man, elderly, and seemingly frail as a
sparrow, though he must have had enormous reserves of
stamina on which to draw.

Behind him, sheltering in the leeside of the Spirit of the Lord
as it blustered and rushed through Grandpa, my little brother
and I kept score. When the spirit moved, Grandpa shouted
hallelujah in his fine Welsh voice. The shock waves hit Mr.
Peabody sharply in the nape of his neck and travelled down his
spine with such force that he would rise an inch or two from
the pew. Most of his body would go rigid, but his head and his
hands would quiver for seconds at a time. *Glory, glory,* he
would murmur in a terror-stricken prayerful voice.

These seismic interludes infused Sundays with extraordinary
interest. And there was also this: from monitoring the passions
of Mr. Peabody, my brother and I learned self-control, the
ability to tamp down an explosion of mirth and turn it into a
mere telegraphed signal of gleaming eyes and a coded
numerology of fingers.

But then came the day that a shaft of sunlight fell from a

high amberglass window in the church and placed a crown of gold on Mr. Peabody's head. "Oh!" I gasped aloud. *"Look!"* And Grandpa shouted *Hallelujah*! and Mr. Peabody rose up into his corona like a skyrocket and I saw a million golden doves and the gilded petals of all the dahlias in the world rising up into the pointed arch above in which God lived.

"It was the Holy Spirit you saw," the pastor told me. "The Holy Spirit descending as a dove."

"Going *up*," I corrected. "Lots and lots of them, and dahlias too."

"The Holy Spirit," he said again, less certainly. "In the form of a dove."

"I'm not so sure," my Sunday School teacher said. "She makes things up."

"Out of the mouths of babes," the pastor reminded her.

"She makes things up," my Sunday School teacher insisted. "She handles the truth very carelessly. She believes her own lies."

"Grandpa," I asked, "how can you tell the difference between truth and a lie?"

He was working bonemeal into the soil around his dahlias; over us nodded those heavy salmon suns. He went on kneading the rich black loam, intent on his labor.

Apprehensively I persisted: "Is the Morgan Nugget true?"

He went on sifting the soil.

I thought hopefully: perhaps he made up death.

"The truth," he said at last, "shall make you free. John, chapter 8, verse 32."

"Grandpa," I said, "there were doves with gold wings, and dahlias too. Mr. Peabody made them fly. I saw them."

"I know you did."

I leaned towards him. "And the Morgan Nugget?" I breathed.

"Is true," he said. "Is true."

AFTER LONG ABSENCE

FOR YEARS IT HAS BRANCHED extravagantly in dreams, but the mango tree outside the kitchen window in Brisbane is even greener than the jubilant greens of memory. I could almost believe my mother has been out there with spit and polish, buffing up each leaf for my visit. I suggest this to her and she laughs, handing me a china plate.

Her hands are a bright slippery pink from the soap suds and the fierce water, and when I take the plate it is as though I have touched the livid element of a stove. In the nick of time, I grunt something unintelligible in lieu of swearing. "Oh heck," I mumble, cradling the place and my seared fingers in the tea-towel. "I'd forgotten." And we both laugh. It is one of those family idiosyncrasies, an heirloom of sorts, passed down with the plate itself which entered family history on my grand-mother's wedding day. The women in my mother's family have always believed that dishwashing water should be just on the leeside of boiling, and somehow, through sheer conviction that cleanliness is next to godliness, I suppose, their hands can calmly swim in it.

I glance at the wall above the refrigerator, and yes, the needlepoint text is still there, paler from another decade of sun, but otherwise undiminished: *He shall try you in a refiner's fire*.

"Do you still have your pieces?" my mother asks.

DISLOCATIONS

She means the cup, saucer, and plate from my grandmother's dinner set, which is of fine bone china, but Victorian, out of fashion. The heavy band of black and pale orange and gold leaf speaks of boundaries that cannot be questioned.

"I'd never part with it," I say.

And I realize from the way in which she smiles and closes her eyes that she has been afraid it would be one more thing I would have jettisoned. I suppose it seems rather arbitrary to my parents, what I have rejected and what I have hung onto. My mother is suspended there, dishmop in hand, eyes closed, for several seconds. She is "giving thanks". I think with irritation: nothing has ever been secular in this house. Not even the tiniest thing.

"Leave this," my mother says, before I am halfway through the sensation of annoyance. "I'll finish. You sit outside and get some writing done."

And I think helplessly: It's always been like this, a seesaw of frustration and tenderness. Whose childhood and adolescence could have been more stifled or more pampered?

"But I *like* doing this with you," I assure her. "I really do." She smiles and "gives thanks" again, a fleeting and exasperating and totally unconscious gesture. "Honestly," I add, precisely because it has suddenly become untrue, because my irritation has surged as quixotically as the Brisbane River in flood. "It's one of . . ." but I decide not to add that it is one of the few things we can do in absolute harmony.

"You should enjoy the sun while you can," she says. Meaning: before you go back to those unimaginable Canadian winters. "Besides, you'll want to write your letters." She pauses awkwardly, delicately avoiding the inexplicable fact that the others have not yet arrived. She cannot imagine a circumstance that would have taken her away, even temporarily, from her husband and children. All her instincts tell her that such action is negligent and immoral. But she will make no judgments, regardless of inner cost. "And then," she says valiantly, "there's your book. You shouldn't be wasting time

. . . You should get on with your book." My book, which they fear will embarrass them again. My book, which will cause them such pride and bewilderment and sorrow. "Off with you," she says. "Sun's waiting."

I've been back less than twenty-four hours and already I'm dizzy – the same old roller-coaster of anger and love. I surrender the damp linen tea-towel which is stamped with the coats of arms of all the Australian states. I gather up notepad and pen, and head for the sun.

◇◇◇

They are old comforters, the sun and the mango tree. I think I've always been pagan at heart, a sun worshipper, perhaps all Queensland children are. There was always far more solace in the upper branches of this tree than in the obligatory family Bible reading and prayers that followed dinner. I wrap my arms around the trunk, I press my cheek to the rough bark, remembering that wasteland of time, the fifth grade.

I can smell it again, sharp and bitter, see all the cruel young faces. The tree sap still stinks of it. My fingers touch scars in the trunk, the blisters of nail heads hammered in long years ago when we read somewhere that the iron improved the mangoes. The rust comes off now on my hands, a dark stain. I am falling down the endless concrete stairs, I feel the pushing again, the kicking, blood coming from somewhere, I can taste that old fear.

I reach for the branch where I hid; lower now, it seems – which disturbs me. Not as inaccessibly safe as I had thought.

Each night, the pale face of my brother would float from behind the glass of his isolation ward and rise through the mango leaves like a moon. I never asked, I was afraid to ask, "Will he die?" And the next day at school, and the next, I remember, remember: all the eyes pressed up against my life, staring, mocking, hostile, menacing.

There was a mark on me.

I try now to imagine myself as one of the others. I suppose I would simply have seen what they saw: someone dipped in death, someone trailing a shadowy cloak of contamination, someone wilfully dangerous. Why should I blame them that they had to ward me off?

This had, in any case, been foretold.

I had known we were strange from my earliest weeks in the first grade. "The nurse has arrived with your needles," our teacher said, and everyone seemed to know what she was talking about. "You'll go when your name is called. It doesn't hurt."

"It does so," called out Patrick Murphy, and was made to stand in the corner.

"With a name like that," said the teacher, "I'm not surprised."

She was busy unfurling and smoothing out the flutter of consent letters which we had all dutifully returned from home, some of us arriving with the letters safety-pinned to our pinafores. The teacher singled out one of the slips, her brow furrowed.

"I see we have our share of religious fanatics," she said. She began to prowl between the desks, waving the white letter like a flag. "Someone in our class," she announced, "is a killer." She stopped beside my desk and I could smell her anger, musky and acrid and damp. It was something I recognized, having smelled it when our cat was playing with a bird, though I could not have said what part of the smell came from which creature. The teacher put her finger on my shoulder, a summons, and I followed to the front of the class. "This person," said the teacher, "is our killer."

And everyone, myself included, solemnly observed. I looked at my hands and feet, curious. A killer, I thought, tasting the double *l* with interest and terror, my tongue forward against the roof of my mouth.

"Irresponsible! Morally irresponsible!" The teacher's voice was like that of our own pastor when he climbed into the pulpit. She was red in the face. I waited for her, my first victim, to go up in smoke. "Ignorant fanatics," she said, "you and your family. You're the kind who cause an epidemic."

I always remembered the word, not knowing what it meant. I saw it as dark and cumulous, freighted with classroom awe, a bringer of lightning bolts. *Epidemic.* I sometimes credit that moment with the birth of my passionate interest in the pure sound of arrangements of syllables. *Epidemic.* And later, of course, in the fifth grade, *diphtheria*, a beautiful word, but deadly.

I know a lot about words, about their sensuous surfaces, the way the tongue licks at them. And about the depth charges they carry.

My mother brings tea and an Arnott's biscuit, though I have been out here scarcely an hour, and though I have not written a word. I have been sitting here crushing her ferns, my back against the mango tree, remembering Patrick Murphy: how no amount of standings-in-the-corner or of canings (I can hear the surf-like whisper of the switch against his bare calves) could put a dent in his exuberance or his self-destructive honesty.

Once, in the first grade, he retrieved my shoes from the railway tracks where Jimmy Simpson had placed them. In the fifth grade he was sometimes able to protect me, and word reached me that one of his black eyes was on my account. One day I brought him home, and my parents said later they had always believed that some Catholics would be saved, that some were among the Lord's Anointed in spite of rank superstition and the idols in their churches. But I was not seriously encouraged to hope that Patrick Murphy would be in the company of this elect. When my mother offered him homemade lemonade, he told her it beat the bejesus out of the stuff you could get at the shops. He also said that most of the kids at school were full of ratshit and that only one or two sheilas made the place any better than buggery.

One morning Patrick Murphy and I woke up and it was time for high school. We went to different ones, and lost touch, though I saw him one Friday night in the heart of Brisbane, on the corner of Adelaide and Albert Streets, outside the Commonwealth Bank. The Tivoli and the Wintergarden ("dens of iniquity," the pastor said) were emptying and he was part of that crowd, his brushback flopping into his eyes, a girl on his arm. The girl was stunning in a sleazy kind of way: close-fitting slacks and spike heels, a tight sweater, platinum blonde hair and crimson lips. My kind of sheila, I imagined Patrick Murphy grinning, and the thought of his mouth on hers disturbed me. I rather imagined that an extra dollop of original sin came with breasts like hers. I rather hoped so.

I was praying Patrick Murphy wouldn't see me.

From my very reluctant spot in the circle, I could see that his eyes were wholly on his girl's cleavage. I moved slightly, so that my back was to the footpath, but so that I could still see him from out of the corner of my eye. Our circle, which took up two parking spaces, was bisected by the curb outside the Commonwealth Bank. There were perhaps fifteen of us ranged around a woman who sat on a folding chair and hugged a piano accordion. We all had a certain *look*, which was as identifiable in its own way as the look of Patrick Murphy's sheila. My dress was . . . well, *ladylike*, I wore flat heels, I might as well have been branded. I hoped only that my face (unspoiled, as our pastor would have said, by the devil's paintbox) might blend indistinguishably with the colourless air.

At the moment of Patrick Murphy's appearance, my father had the megaphone in his hand and was offering the peace that passeth understanding to all the lost who rushed hither and thither before us, not knowing where they were going.

The theatregoers, their sense of direction thus set at nought, appeared to me incandescent with goodwill, the light of weekend in their eyes. I (for whom Friday night was the most dreaded night of a circumscribed week) watched them as a starving waif might peer through a restaurant window.

"I speak not of the pleasures of this world, which are fleeting," my father said through the megaphone. "Not as the world giveth, give I unto you . . . ."

Patrick Murphy and his sheila had drawn level with the Commonwealth Bank. Dear God, I prayed, let the gutter swallow me up. Let the heavens open. Let not Patrick Murphy see me.

Patrick Murphy stopped dead in his tracks and a slow grin of recognition lit his face. I squirmed with mortal shame, I could feel the heat rash on my cheeks.

"Jesus," laughed his sheila, snapping her gum. "Will ya look at those Holy Rollers."

"They got guts," said Patrick Murphy. "I always did go for guts," and he gave me the thumbs-up sign with a wink and a grin.

At Wallace Bishop's Diamond Arcade, he turned back to blow me a kiss.

It was the last time I saw him before he hitched his motorcycle to the tailgate of a truck and got tossed under its sixteen double tyres. This happened on the Sandgate Road, near Nudgee College, and the piece in the *Courier-Mail* ran a comment by one of the priests. A bit foolhardy, perhaps, Father O'Shaughnessy said, a bit of a daredevil. Yet a brave lad, just the same, and a good one at heart. Father O'Shaughnessy could vouch for this, although he had not had the privilege, etcetera. But the lad was wearing a scapular around his neck.

Rest in peace, Patrick Murphy, I murmur, making a cross in the dust with a mango twig.

"What are you doing?" my mother asks, smelling liturgical errors.

"Doodling. Just doodling." But certain statues in churches – the Saint Peters, the faulty impetuous saints – have always had Patrick Murphy's eyes.

❖❖❖

A few minutes later, my mother is back. "We've had a call from Miss Martin's niece in Melbourne. You remember Miss Martin? Her niece is worried. Miss Martin isn't answerng her phone so we're going over." They call out from the car: "She still lives in Red Hill, we won't be long."

Miss Martin was old when I was a child. She's ninety-eight now, part of the adopted family, a network of the elderly, the lonely, the infirm, the derelict. My parents collect them. It has always been like this, and I've lost count of how many there are: people they check in on, they visit, they sit with, they take meals to. My mother writes letters for ladies with crippled arthritic hands and mails them to distant relatives who never visit. She has a long inventory of birthdays to be celebrated, she takes little gifts and cakes with candles.

By mid-afternoon she calls. "We're at the hospital. We got to her just in time. Do you mind getting your own dinner? I think we should stay with her, she'll be frightened when she regains consciousness."

They keep vigil throughout the night.

At dawn the phone wakes me. "She's gone," my mother says. "The Lord called her to be with Himself. Such a peaceful going home."

The day after the funeral, my father and I drive out to the university.

"It's not easy," he says, "trying to get a B.A. at my age."

But there is pride, just the same, in this mad scheme I have talked him into. I have always thought of him as an intellectual *manqūe* whose life was interfered with by the Depression and the Gospel – (His aunts in Adelaide never recovered from the distress. "Oh your father," they said to me sadly, shaking their heads. "He was led astray." By my mother's family, they meant. "We do wish he hadn't been taken in by such a . . . We do wish he would come back to a *respectable* religion.") – and whose retirement is now interfered with by all the lives that must be succoured and sustained. "It's hard to find time to study," he confesses ruefully.

People will keep on dying, or otherwise needing him.

In the university library, he leafs through books like an acolyte who has at last – after a lifetime of longing – been permitted to touch the holy objects. He strokes them with work-knotted fingers. But we are simply passing through the library today, we are on our way to meet friends of mine for lunch at the staff club. I am privately apprehensive about this, though my father is delighted, curious, secretly flattered. He has never been in a staff club lounge.

At the table reserved for us the waiter is asking, "red or white, sir?" and my heart sinks. The air is full of greeting and reminiscence, but I am waiting for my father's inevitable gesture, the equivalent of the megaphone outside the Commonwealth Bank. I am bracing myself to stay calm, knowing I will be as angered by the small patronizing smiles of my old friends as by my father's compulsion to "bear witness". He will turn his wineglass upside down at the very least; possibly he will make some mild moral comment on drink; he may offer the peace that passeth understanding to the staff club at large.

He does none of these things.

To my astonishment, he permits the waiter to fill his glass with white wine. He is bemused, I decide, by his surroundings. And yet twice during the course of the meal, he takes polite sips from his glass.

The magnitude of this gesture overwhelms me. I have to excuse myself from the table for ten minutes.

❖❖❖

For a week I have cunningly avoided being home with my parents for dinner, but the moment of reckoning has come. We are all here, brothers and sisters-in-law and nieces and nephews, an exuberantly affectionate bunch.

The table has been cleared now, and my father has reached for the Bible. A pause. I feel like a gladiator waiting for the lions, all the expectant faces turned towards me. It is time. The visitor always chooses the Bible reading, the visitor reads; and then my father leads family prayer.

It should be a small thing. In anyone else's home I would endure it with docile politeness.

It cannot be a concession anywhere near as great as my father's two sips of wine – a costly self-damning act.

It should be a small thing for me to open the Bible and read. There is no moral principle at stake.

Yet I cannot do it.

"I am sorry," I say quietly, hating myself.

Outside I hug the mango tree and weep for the kind of holy innocence that can inflict appalling damage; and because it is clear that they, the theologically rigid, are more forgiving than I am.

But I also move out of the shaft of light that falls from the house, knowing, with a rush of annoyance, that if they see me weeping they will discern the Holy Spirit who hovers always with his bright demanding wings.

I lean against the dark side of the mango tree and wait. A flying fox screeches in the banana clump. Gloating, the Holy Spirit whispers: *Behold the foxes, the little foxes, that spoil the vines*. One by one, the savaged bananas fall, thumping softly on the grass. From the window the sweet evening voices drift out in a hymn. The flying fox, above me, arches his black gargoyle wings.